STALLED INDEPENDENCE

Holidays in Lake Point 3

Sarah Cass

Sensual Romance
Mainstream Romance

Sarah Cass
www.authorsarahcass.com

Divine Roses Ink Publishing
www.divinerosesink.com

A Divine Roses Ink Book
Sensual Romance
Mainstream Romance
Stalled Independence
Copyright © 2014 Sarah Cass
Second E-book Publication: September 2015
First E-book Publication: June 2014

Cover design by Sarah Cass
Edited by Megan Koenen
Proofread by Belinda Barton
All cover art and logo copyright © 2014 by Sarah Cass

PUBLISHER
Divine Roses Ink
http://www.divinerosesink.com

Books by Sarah Cass
The Tribe Series
The Tribe
The Wolf
The Chief
The Raven
The Dominion Falls Series
Changing Tracks
Derailed
Dark Territory
Runaway Train
Home Signal
The Lake Point Series
Santa, Maybe
Deep-Fried Sweethearts
Stalled Independence
Witch Way
A Thorough Thanksgiving
Eve's New Year
Heartstrings & Hockey Pucks
Luck of the Cowgirl
Stars, Stripes & Motorbikes
Free Falling
Love for Hire
Stand Alone Novels
Masked Hearts
Leap

Dedication

This story is dedicated to all the women like Regan.
To those that had a Grace in their lives, and most
especially to those who don't.
I hope you find your way out.
I hope you find your way home.

Chapter One

"No, not here," Regan whined. The car sputtered and spurted. It barely made it to the shoulder before dying. She hit the steering wheel hard, like that would do her any good, and dropped her forehead to the wheel.

Tears she'd managed to keep at bay for almost the entire day welled up again. She had no idea where she was, other than New York. The last few signs had said something about Rochester, but she'd passed those signs twenty minutes ago.

She lifted her head, wiping the tears from her eyes so she could see. The road sign ahead read 'Lake Point. 1 mile'. A groan escaped and she dropped her head to the steering wheel. A solid thump resonated through her already pounding head, taking the decibel level of her headache to near migraine levels. "What am I going to do?"

There was nowhere left to go. She'd had no destination in mind, and should've been grateful the car had taken her this far away from her home state of Illinois.

A shuddering breath racked her lungs and a sob tore from her gut. For three days, she'd driven all over the place. She didn't want to follow a straight line, and that left her lost in more ways than one.

Oh, who was she kidding? She'd been lost for years. Her actual location no longer mattered.

A sharp knock on the window startled a shriek out of her.

"Ma'am? Y'all right in there? Do you need a hand?" Another tap on her window drew her toward the window and the—the fricking cowboy standing outside.

A cowboy? In New York? Her hands shook too hard to move, and she imagined she looked frightful. The way his eyes widened didn't lessen that belief. She pressed down her lock and nodded. "I'm fine. Go away. Please. I'll call someone."

"Sorry I startled you, Miss." A smile broke on the disturbingly handsome face. "Name's Clay. It's right smart of you not to open up. You got someone to call?"

No, she didn't. Worse, the pay-as-you-go phone she'd bought was dead after her last call to Grace. At this point in time, she had no one to help her. No one but the man outside her window, but she wasn't about to get out and hitch a ride with a perfect stranger.

"How about I call Sheriff Calvin? And I'll call for a tow and have the car taken to my garage." Clay apparently took her silence for an acknowledgement that she didn't know what to do. He took out his phone and dialed.

All she could do was nod rapidly, even though he'd turned away. She had no idea what else would work. Her voice didn't want to function, and the world had crashed in when the car died. The reality of what she'd done, and how alone she was now, dug at the dark hole in her soul until her lip trembled again.

Thankfully the cowboy backed off and went back to his truck, still focused on his phone. It left her free to try to gather herself together. She turned the rear-view mirror toward herself and let out a bitter laugh. Red splotched her face, the damnable dark circles under her eyes a deep purple now that the makeup had all been cried and wiped away.

She sniffled and wiped at her cheeks to remove the last salty vestiges of the 'hysterical woman' she'd so often been accused of being. At this point, maybe, she should have felt relief, but she felt more scared than ever.

Flashing lights came into view at the edge of her mirror and she shifted it back to get a better view. A cop car had pulled up behind Clay and the sheriff now stood shaking the man's hand. So, he wasn't a homicidal maniac, or if he was he was a damn good one.

A strangled laugh choked out at that ridiculous thought and she cleared her throat. After a long exhale and a shake to remove the last of her nerves, she unlocked the door again. By the time the cop got to her car, she felt somewhat composed, even if she looked like hell.

"Everything all right, miss?" The short man stood at the ready, one hand on his holster, apparently just in case she was the homicidal maniac. Not that she blamed him after the show she'd just put on, which Clay must have told him about. No wonder Tony always said she was too emotional.

The mere thought of him brought up a whimper so fast she couldn't stop it. Luckily, it wasn't a full-on sob, and she was able to nod. "My car broke down. I've got no one to call. I'm just…"

"It's okay. Clay's already called a tow for you. If anyone can fix this, he can. I'm sure your car is perfectly fine." The man reeked of doubt when he took in the car. It was a heap of junk, and she knew it. "How about I give you a ride to the garage? You can wait for it there."

There wasn't anything else to do. Short of finding another heap of junk that would wipe her out of the last bit of money she had. If there was a higher power, it was telling her to stop where she was. Well, message received. With a long sigh, she shrugged. "I suppose. So he's okay?"

Sheriff Calvin glanced back to the truck and snorted. "Clay? He's harmless. Don't bite or nothing. Damn good with cars, too. Don't let the cowboy thing freak you out. We try not to."

She allowed an uneasy laugh and grabbed her purse. Once she stepped out, she took a deep breath. "Thank you."

"No problem. I'm Sheriff Calvin, but most people just call me Calvin. And this here is Clay Ryley." Calvin gestured to the cowboy.

Clay tipped his hat. "Sorry again about startling you, Miss. I saw you stall out and thought I'd try to help."

"I appreciate it. Sorry for, well, this." She gestured to her face. "It's been a long drive."

"No problem. You go on with Calvin. I'll wait for the truck."

She nodded and let the sheriff lead her toward his car. Before she got in, she chanced another glance at the cowboy. Figures on the one day in her life she met a hot cowboy she was a total wreck. Death warmed over probably looked better.

With a sigh, she slid into the car and pulled her purse tight against her chest.

* * * *

Clay left the hood up on the car even though he knew there was nothing to be done for the hunk of junk the girl had been driving. To be honest, he had no idea how far she'd managed to make it in the thing, but he was shocked it had gone anywhere.

He lifted his hat to scratch his forehead when Cal stepped out of the office. "What's the word, Cal?"

"I was going to ask you the same thing." Cal leaned against the quarter panel. "Not that I even have to ask. Where did she find this?"

"No idea. Probably the same place it's going to end up— a junkyard. She might get a couple hundred bucks out of it." Clay set the hat back on his head. "Hate to tell her that. It looks like she's been in some hard times."

"Sure seems that way. Says her name is Regan. Far as I can tell she's got nowhere to stay. And from the way she talked, I'm not even sure she knew where she was going."

"Her plate says Wyoming. That's a long way to come without knowing where you're going."

"You're telling me. I'm going to run across the street and get some food for her at The Diner. Her stomach was growling while we were talking."

Clay nodded. "That's fine. I'll go on up and tell her what's going on with her car. She'll need a place to stay until she has a way to get moving again. With tourist season started, the Neeley's place is a no-go, but I'll check with Ryan over at the Lakeside Motel and see if he has a room available for her."

"Sounds like a plan. Just don't go scaring the poor girl again." Cal grinned. "She had no idea what to make of a cowboy in the middle of New York State."

"Most people don't." Clay laughed and waved as Cal left. With a frown, he sighed and turned to glance into his office again.

Inside, she sat on the couch with the tip of her thumb pinched between her teeth as she stared at the phone on the desk. She closed her eyes and her shoulders drooped. She sagged back against the back of the couch, her thumb dropping from her mouth.

Clay slipped to the stairs and hopped up them. His boots clanged on the metal intentionally, and had the desired effect as Regan startled and sat straighter. Last thing he wanted to do was scare her again.

When he opened the door, she rose, rubbing her palms against the thighs of her jeans. She nodded and managed a smile. "Hi."

"Hey." Clay left the office door open and sat on the edge of his desk. "Cal tells me your name is Regan."

"Yes. And the car?"

"I'm afraid it's done for. To be honest, I'm surprised it made it from Wyoming with the size of the hole in the radiator, not to mention the huge oil leak."

Her brow puckered and she sank back onto the couch. "I just needed something that ran, and it did. Until it didn't."

"I can't believe it ran at all."

"Neither could the guy at the junkyard." A cross between a smirk and a grimace pinched her features until she smoothed into stoicism. "I guess I stay here, then."

Clay blinked and shook his head. "I'm sorry?"

"Oh." A hint of pink seeped into her cheeks. "Well, when I bought the car, we said I'd go as far as the car would take me. Where it died, is where I'd stay."

"We?"

"I. I mean, I."

"Well, either way, that's an interesting philosophy."

"Sometimes you need a fresh start, you know?" She sighed, her gaze fixed on the car outside. "That doesn't mean I have the faintest idea how."

"I get the need to start over. Think everyone's felt that way at some point. Not easy to do on your own, though." He smiled. "You didn't think about what you'd want to do?"

"You'd think I would— it's not like I didn't have time." She twitched her lips. "But there isn't much I'm qualified for."

Clay crossed his ankles and studied her. So many questions he wanted to ask, but none felt anywhere near appropriate. So instead, he chose to remain with a safe topic. "Not much? What do you like to do?"

"What I like to do isn't worth anything. I'll have to do what I can to make a living, I suppose." She turned her full attention on him, her tawny brown eyes rimmed in tears. "I've worked in a book shop, and as a waitress."

"Did someone say waitress?" Myrtle Montague interrupted Clay's attempt to gather a response. The older woman climbed the four steps into his office with a smile. "Clay. How are you?"

He accepted her hug and kissed her cheek when she turned it up toward him. With his own family still back in South Carolina, Myrtle and her nephew, Tag, were the closest things he had to family in Lake Point. She had him over every Thanksgiving, and always expressed sadness that he would go home for Christmas. "I'm great, Myrtle. You?"

"Doing well. Can't complain." Myrtle lifted the bag she'd carried in. "Cal got called to duty, so I thought I'd bring over food for the young lady here myself, and I brought you some too, Clay."

"Not a beef Manhattan!" He could smell the gravy before she'd lifted the box out of the bag. "You are trying to make me fat."

Myrtle laughed and smacked his stomach. "I don't think that's possible, my boy. Now," Myrtle turned toward Regan, "on to you. It's good to meet you, child."

Regan's eyes widened. After a moment, she shook off whatever had bothered her and rose. "Hi. I'm Regan."

"So I've heard." Myrtle reached into the bag and pulled out another to-go carton. When Clay reached toward the bag and the smaller boxes filled, as always, with desserts, Myrtle smacked his hand. "Eat your lunch first, Mr. Ryley."

"Yes ma'am." Clay dropped into the closest chair and popped open his lunch.

"I also heard you came a long way. Wyoming?" Myrtle handed Regan the box of food. "This is my lunch special today. Barbeque bacon cheeseburger and some piping hot fries. I put some ketchup in there for you, too."

Regan's stomach growled, and Clay could have sworn she licked her lips. "I love barbeque bacon cheeseburgers. Thank you so much. How much do I owe you?"

"Don't you worry none. First one's on the house. Now, sit. Eat."

Regan didn't wait to be told twice. She dropped back down on the couch and dug into her burger without hesitation.

"Tell me what you're doing here in Lake Point."

She took a big bite and swallowed before answering. "I was just passing through."

He couldn't deny his amusement at her lack of effort to put on airs of dainty, birdlike eating. Whether because she was starving or not, it was great. "Myrtle makes a damn good burger."

Regan's deep moan of agreement through another big bite caught him off-guard, and his cock twitched. He coughed at the surprise reaction, dropping his gaze so he could regain control of his libido.

"Wow. That's so good." Regan grabbed three fries together and raked them through the ketchup. "I could die happy after this burger."

"Well, hopefully it won't come to that." Myrtle laughed. "So, you were passing through?"

"That was the plan, but my car had other ideas." After gesturing toward the junk pile of a car in the garage, Regan bit off the ketchup-dipped ends of her fries. "So, since I'd planned to stay wherever the car died, I guess, I'm here."

"Well, darling, why are you here instead of home?" Myrtle shook her head. "What about your Mama?"

Clay lost his appetite when Regan's usually animated features fell into a mask. There was clearly more to her situation than she was letting on.

Regan set aside her fries and grabbed her burger. "We haven't talked in a long time. I really didn't have anything left for me back in Illinois." She took a huge bite as if to keep from having to talk again.

"Illinois?" Clay leaned forward. "Your license plate says Wyoming."

Regan nodded and wiped some sauce from the corner of her mouth. "It came with the car. I wasn't supposed to talk about that. Shoot."

"Wasn't supposed to talk about what?" Myrtle set her hand on Regan's. "Are you in some sort of trouble?"

"No." Even Regan knew she'd answered too quickly, if her return to the deer-in-the-headlights look was any indication. "I mean, I'm not a criminal or anything. I just, had to get away. There wasn't anything in Illinois for me anymore."

Myrtle's brow furrowed, but she nodded and sat straighter. "Fair enough. I know what that's like myself. Now eat up, I'll stop making you talk so you can finish. I brought some apple pie to have for dessert."

Regan's shoulders sagged and she dove back into her burger.

Clay exchanged glances with Myrtle, but didn't say a word. While Regan ate heartily, Clay picked at his food. Myrtle bustled about, cleaning up his office, and he knew better than to tell her to stop. She wasn't one to sit still, but she likely wasn't going to leave until she could be sure Regan was going to be taken care of.

When Regan closed the take-out box and set it aside, she sighed again. She stopped to lick the barbeque sauce from her fingers, and Clay had to look away again.

What is your problem? Clay closed his own food box and rubbed his hand over his face. Usually he had enough control, or maybe disinterest, to not get turned on by everything a woman did. He'd heard of love at first sight, but this was more like lust at first sight. Nothing like that had happened since his freshman year of college.

"I'm sorry, did you say pie?" Regan offered a sheepish grin. "I'm a sucker for any kind of pie but rhubarb."

"That's just because you haven't had my rhubarb pie." Myrtle took out one of the pie boxes and handed it off along with a plastic fork. "Here you go."

"Thank you." Regan plucked some crust off the top. "Do either of you know where I could stay for at least a few days? Maybe longer?"

"I was going to call Ryan for you. He runs the Lakeside Motel right up the road. Tourist season is just starting, so I'm sure he still has a room available." Clay slipped his food under his chair, he'd eat it later. "As for what you do after that, I'm sure we can find you a job and a more permanent place to stay for a while."

"I have some money." Regan ate three bites of pie after her declaration. When no one spoke into the silence, she swallowed and sighed. "But I'll need to find a job of some kind."

"Weren't you saying something about waitressing when I got here?" Myrtle perched on the edge of Clay's desk. "I could use a good waitress across the street."

"Really?" Regan's eyes were wide. "I wasn't digging for a job. I'd work hard, I don't want you to give me a job because you feel sorry for me or anything."

"Now who said anything like that?" Myrtle scoffed. "I don't give anyone a free ride, child. Not even my own kin. I just had a waitress turn in her notice, so the timing is perfect."

"She's not kidding," Clay added when Regan set aside her pie under the chastising. "She wouldn't even give Tag a job; he had to find one on his own."

"You hush." Myrtle chuckled. "Why don't you get yourself settled in the motel and come see me tomorrow? We'll do a proper interview and see if it's a fit."

Once again, the tension in Regan's shoulders seemed to seep away. "That sounds good, thanks."

"Don't thank me yet. I haven't actually hired you yet."

Chapter Two

Regan tapped the phone card against her thigh, slid her fingers down the length and flipped it. Over and over she repeated the process as she stared at the hotel phone.

After several minutes, she grabbed the phone and began the long-drawn-out dialing process. Tension kept her shoulders taut until she heard Grace's voice on the other end of the line. "Thank you for calling DCNB. This is Grace, how may I help you save today?"

"Grace?" Regan's voice cracked. After she'd cleared her throat, she took a deep breath. "Grace, it's me."

"Amanda?" Grace practically whispered into the phone. "Hold on."

Regan flinched at the use of her real first name. When she'd left home she'd changed it, on Grace's recommendation, but there'd been no time to tell Grace what she'd picked. She resumed tapping her card against her thigh and chewed her lip while she waited. Over the line she could hear a door close, and then the static of the headset moving.

"Amanda, how are you?" Grace sighed. "I was worried about you."

"The phone died, the car died." Regan let out a shaky breath. "And I'm going by Regan here. I always liked it better anyway."

"Regan is better for me." Grace chuckled. "I can say that without everyone trying to be nosy about where you went."

"I'm in—"

"No. Don't tell me," Grace interrupted. "Tony's been by here every day. I like to keep my denial believable. I don't want to know where you are, but I am glad to know you're safe."

"I am. I think. I don't have a car, but luckily, I don't think I'll need to use one." Regan leaned against the headboard. The rest of her tension seeped away. "I already found a job. My boss is real nice, said she'd keep her ears out for an inexpensive place to live."

"You don't sound too sure."

"I just…"

"It's tougher actually stopping where the car dies than it sounds, isn't it?" Grace's understanding tone soothed the last of Regan's tension. "I remember, but I made it through when I left my man, and you will too. That's why we got you a junker. The sooner it died, the better. You still have money left now, right?"

"I do. Enough for a security deposit and first month's rent if I find something soon. The guy at the body shop is seeing what he can get to scrap the car for me." She chewed her lip, afraid to ask the question she couldn't push aside no matter how hard she tried.

"That's good."

"Grace. Is Tony…"

"You deserve better. Take out the pictures now. Look at what he did to you. Remember why you left. He wasn't going to stop."

Regan screwed her eyes shut and shook her head. "No. I can't."

"Do it. He doesn't need your concern. He didn't give you any."

"Seven years, Grace. It's not that easy to forget I loved him once."

"That wasn't love, sweetie. You were sixteen when you two started dating. It wasn't love, it was something else—and what it became after was definitely not love, either."

"I know, I know." So many times they'd had this discussion. For months before the first time Tony had hit her, Grace had known how Regan's relationship had been.

"So don't you worry about him. Worry about yourself. Whenever you feel weak, take out the picture. You promised you would."

"I know. I will." Regan took a deep, ragged breath. A knock at the door startled her from her next sentence. She frowned and rose to peek out the curtains.

Outside her door stood Clay. Once again she was taken aback by the cowboy appearance. His large hat left his face in shadow, but she remembered the kind, slate gray eyes. Even after her hysterical outburst the day before, everything about him had been caring, even gentle. Of course, she'd have to be blind to not notice the way his jeans clung to his long, lean legs.

"They don't make them like that back home." She sighed.

"What?" Grace's voice reminded Regan that she was still on the phone. "Regan, what are you talking about?"

"Uh, oh. It's the cowboy—I mean, it's the mechanic. Probably here with the scrap estimate." Heat rose to Regan's cheeks, and she had to wipe her sweaty palms on her thighs.

"Cowboy? I'll want to know more. For now, I should get back to work. Denny has passed by three times to peek in here and check on me." Grace sighed. "Call me next time after work on my cell. We'll talk more."

"Okay, Grace. Thanks again." Regan set the phone down on the table and rushed to the door. When she flung it open, Clay had turned to leave and she got a perfect view of how well his jeans fit, and never before had she admired an ass quite as much as she did this one. *What are you thinking? Last thing you need now is any guy. Then again, there's no crime against looking.*

A hand waved in front of her face and a whistle drew her attention back to the matter at hand. Clay offered a grin that would have melted her heart if she ever dared dream a man like him could want anything to do with her. After a second, he chuckled. "So I don't get a how-do?"

"Oh, damn. Sorry. I'm still getting used to this whole cowboy thing."

"I'm used to that." He laughed. "Mind if I come in? Or do you want to talk out here?"

Regan dared a glance at her room, which she'd already turned into a clutter-bomb of chaos. After a sigh, she shook her head. "Give me a second. I was actually going to walk the square and grab a bite to eat. Let me grab my purse, if you don't mind walking with me."

"I sure don't mind one bit." He tipped his hat. "Take your time. I'll be right here."

She closed the door and darted to the bathroom to double check her make up. Once there, she frowned, running her fingers over her cheeks and under her eyes. All her flaws stared back like they had neon signs over them.

Too-round cheeks. Too-thin top lip. Eyes more hazel than a deep-rich brown like her mother's. Dark circles under her eyes only partly hidden by make-up. She sighed and Tony's voice rang through her head. *You think you can do better? Please. Look at yourself.*

She backed away from the mirror and left the room, her ego deflated. Clay was probably being so nice and friendly to keep her from bursting into ugly tears again. She knew all too well how frightening her blotchy skin and puffy eyes looked after a good cry.

On her way to the door, she grabbed her purse and tossed it over her shoulder. She ducked her head and stepped outside. Once she'd tested the door to be sure it was locked, she turned toward Clay. Rather than look him in the eye, she kept her focus on the cars passing down Main Street. "I don't want to take you from work."

"I'm on lunch. You okay?"

"Yeah. Fine. I just—it was presumptuous of me to ask you to walk along with me. You have a business to run."

"Like I said, I'm on lunch. I was actually going to head up to the square and eat at The Midway once we'd talked about your car. Do you like carnival food?"

"What?" She was too confused to not meet his gaze. "You have a fair that runs in the beginning of May?"

"No. County fair isn't until July. The Midway is a restaurant on the square. It's a favorite among the kids, all the sweets and bad-for-you goodies Mikey's got on the menu."

Sweets? She wasn't sure she should admit just how much of a sweet tooth she had. For years her mother had warned her that her sweet tooth would catch up with her waist line, but it hadn't happened yet. Regan didn't want to seem too eager. "Is there actual food?"

"Philly cheese steaks, burgers, tenderloins—seriously anything you could find at a fair."

The menu sounded so much more delicious than it should, and her stomach growled in response. "I hate to say it, but it sounds really good. I don't want to intrude on your lunch."

"Stop worrying so much. I get bored eating by myself all the time. Besides, I really want to see your reaction to the place. Mikey went all out on it."

"I've never heard of anything like it." Before she knew it, she was hop stepping to catch up with him as he headed down the street. "Where did he come up with the idea?"

Clay laughed. "Mikey's a she. Sorry, her name's Michaela, but most everyone calls her Mikey. I don't know where she came up with it. Maybe she's just got a big ol' sweet tooth."

"Or she's brilliant."

"Maybe a little of both." Clay laughed as they reached the crosswalk.

While they waited for the light, Regan took in the quaint town square in front of them. Since she'd arrived in town the day before, she hadn't had time to really see the place. Around the square, the town appeared stuck in time. The brick buildings were kept up and clean, and the proud white courthouse stood in the middle. "It reminds me of..."

"Back to the Future?"

She laughed and nodded. "Exactly what I was thinking. It's not quite the same, I mean, the square is smaller, but it's so similar." Even the clocks in the peaks of the courthouse harkened to the clock frozen in time by the lightning strike.

"I noticed it myself when I got to town. I loved the movies."

"You?" Embarrassment struck the moment she said it aloud and she ducked her head.

"Yes, me. I might be a born and raised cowboy," he winked and tipped his hat as his southern lilt took a front seat to tease her, "but you'd be surprised what else I am. I'm not the total cliché. Well, I am, but not just that."

Her curiosity was interrupted by the light changing. They darted across the street. Once they touched sidewalk again, she let her question slip. "So what else are you?"

"Nah, I want you to guess."

"Well, I know you're a mechanic."

"That guess doesn't count." As they passed the movie theater, Clay spun on his heel and walked backward. "One guess."

"Well," she hedged. When he stopped with his hand on the door of the restaurant, her stomach growled, but she still hesitated. Last thing she'd want to do is insult him, but he did ask. *What would be the opposite of a cowboy?*

"Can't have nothing to do with animals. I don't train horses, I just ride 'em. My sister's the trainer." He grinned, leaning against the door handle. She wondered if anyone inside was trying to get out.

"I guess, the opposite of what I'd expect would be some genius scientist."

"Give the girl a cookie." He grinned and pulled open the door. "After you, ma'am."

"What?" She'd never in her life had her jaw literally drop, but as several people passed between them in and out of the restaurant she found she had to physically make her mouth close. "You aren't serious?"

"I am. Now let's get you that cookie. I bet Mikey's got some out on display."

* * * *

Clay had to physically guide Regan inside, and he chuckled the whole time. It had been a while since he'd gotten this reaction. Everyone in town knew he was a scientist, so it didn't shock anyone anymore.

Regan stopped inside the door and her whole body turned in a circle to take in the brightly colored walls covered in graffiti from nearly everyone in town. Off to their right, against the wall, were the carnival games set up for kids and adults alike.

"Like you said. Mikey's a genius. You like it?"

"It's so cool." She laughed. "I thought you were kidding, but carnival games and oh—"

Clay followed her to the candy display. There wasn't anything specifically for the fourth of July yet, but he knew Tag and Mikey were hard at work on something. "In a few weeks they'll have out all holiday-themed candy. Tag and Mikey are both brilliant with sweets."

"It all looks so delicious."

He was glad she'd gotten over her earlier discomfort, and the candy had distracted her from her shock at least temporarily. When Tag himself walked up, Clay grinned. "Hey. You going to get that heap of junk out of my garage any time in the near future?"

"That is no heap of junk." Michaela protested from behind the register a few feet away. "Give us a year and she'll be purring like a kitten and you'll wish she was back in your garage."

Tag laughed. "She's right, Clay. Don't pick on my Nova. You'll miss her when she's gone."

"I still don't believe Mikey has one, and is helping you with yours. Although maybe now it'll actually get done. You're just screwing around; I think Mikey's dead serious." Clay winked in Michaela's direction, then turned his attention to Regan. "Tag, this is Regan. She's going to be working for your aunt."

Regan straightened, her hand still on the case protecting the candy. She blinked a few times and shook her head. A standard reaction when women met Tag, but Clay felt a misplaced spark of jealousy that Regan would react to the young man. Light pink filtered into her cheeks, and she ducked her head again. "I'm sorry. I was distracted by the candy. What?"

"You're working for Auntie M?" Tag leaned on the case. "Oh, you're the girl Clay got to rescue yesterday."

"Myrtle is your aunt?" Regan smiled. "She was good enough to give me a job. Seemed real nice. Honest."

Tag snorted. "That's a nice way to say blunt."

"Clay. What'll it be?" Michaela waved them over once her customers left.

"I'll get my usual, and then whatever Regan wants is on my tab." He shook his head when she started to protest. "Consider it an apology for scaring you yesterday."

Regan placed her order and followed him to the soda machine. Once they were settled at a table, she continued to scan the restaurant. She didn't comment on it, though, she went back to his confession. "So you're a genius scientist?"

"Maybe not a genius."

"Then what would you call it?"

"Smart. I was at RIT for a while working on a dual major."

She plunged her straw in and out of her drink like she was working a butter churn. At his silence, she lifted her golden brown gaze on him. "Well? Your dual majors in what?"

"Physics and Mechanical Engineering."

The straw stopped moving and for the second time her jaw hung open. "Seriously?"

"Yup." Their food arrived and interrupted the conversation again. He dove in without answering the unspoken question. If possible, he wanted to leave it hanging so he'd have to see her again to answer it. Never mind the fact she'd be working right across the street from the shop. "So, your car."

"Oh. Right." She covered her mouth when she realized she'd spoken around her food. Once she swallowed, she nodded. "How bad?"

"Well, you got more out of the pile of scrap metal than I thought you would." Clay popped a fry in his mouth. "I got you two hundred and fifty for it."

Mid-way through her drink, she coughed and set it aside. "Really? I thought I'd get fifty."

"If I'd sold it whole to the junkyard you might have gotten a hundred, but I took out some good scrap metal parts that would fetch more money for their metal alone. The rest went to the junkyard." Clay shrugged and sat back. He'd wanted to help her out as much as he could. Something told him she was lost in more ways than one. "Thought you could use the cash."

"Thank you. Really." She smiled, but tears shimmered at the edge of her eyes. "I can't thank you enough for helping me."

"No need to thank me."

"But you don't even know me. You've done so much. Everyone has."

"You seem surprised. Don't you know nice people?"

Silence greeted his question, and she sat hunched over, dipping her fry repeatedly into her ketchup. She shoved the fry into her mouth, and followed with another bite of burger. Rather than look at him, she scanned the walls.

"Well you do now."

Her lips curled up, but it came out more of a grimace than a smile. "That'll take some getting used to."

"Don't you have any friends?"

"One. Probably not going to see her again, though."

"I think that'll change now. One of the benefits of a small town is you get to know everyone pretty fast, and you have a head start."

She managed to meet his gaze again.

Clay had to resist the urge to take her hand, but he did grin. "You already got one friend."

"I…do?"

"Sure do. Right here. Me." He held up his hand before she could say anything further. "Don't matter that I don't know you too well, that'll come with time. If you're gonna be here a while, we got that."

Her mouth opened and closed like she wanted to protest. Instead, she took another large bite of her burger and ducked her head again.

"So let's start on that, eh? Tell me about yourself. Do you know how to ride horses?"

Whatever surprise or fear she'd been holding onto drained from her shoulders when she snorted. She covered her mouth as she continued to chuckle. Once she'd managed to swallow and take a drink of water she was really laughing. "You want to stick with the cliché, then?"

"Might as well. I look the part." Clay grinned and lifted his hat back onto his head. "I can drawl, too, if you'd like."

"I do kind of like it." She sucked her lips between her teeth, but her laughter kept coming, even if she was embarrassed by the honest statement. "As far as horses go, I haven't in a long time. My aunt used to have a horse farm years ago and I rode then. It's been years and I didn't spend a lot of time there. I do like it, though."

"Good to know. You'll have to see the Neeley's. They run a B&B down the road a piece, and Hank breeds thoroughbreds. They board my horse for me, too."

"Where are you from, originally?"

"Camden, South Carolina. Three sisters; Calliope, Cadence, and Cheyenne. Sensing a theme?"

"One of your parents likes the letter C." She smiled. "All right, I was born in California, but we moved to Illinois when I was fourteen. My brother was in college, so he stayed behind. Just the one brother, and we don't get along."

"Too bad. I'd be lost without my family. We talk all the time." No wonder she seemed lost; she didn't even get along with her brother. "Plus, the family I gained here helps. Tag and Myrtle have become like a second family to me."

"Sounds nice." And she disappeared again. Lost in the depths of her own thoughts, the laughter faded as she went back to eating.

"What about movies?" He was desperate to draw her out again. "What sort of movies do you like?"

"Hate horror movies." She swept the fry into her mouth and sighed. "I'm a bit of a geek. I like *Star Trek, Star Wars*, and *Firefly*. I'm also a total girl. I like the chick flicks. Some westerns, too. I'm a sucker for the series *Deadwood*."

"I love that show. Hated they cancelled it well before its time." Clay grinned. "And I'm a geek, too, just in disguise."

"That's one hell of a disguise, cowboy."

"I know."

Chapter Three

Regan rushed into The Diner so fast she forgot to let go of the door and got yanked backwards. Her finger smarted and she cursed under her breath. "Crap, damn, ow."

"Well there you are, sunshine." Myrtle set two full plates down on the bar for the waiting customers. "I was getting worried about you."

"Sorry. Sorry." Regan shook out her hand and shed her coat. "The alarm in the apartment didn't go off."

"How did your first night in the new place go?"

Thanks to Myrtle, Regan had found a nice, small, and furnished apartment to rent that wasn't too expensive. Although it was someone's finished basement, she had a front and back door, a kitchen and bathroom. Her bedroom and living room were the same room, but there was a large walk-in closet that would have been great if she still had all her clothes. "It was okay."

"Just okay?" Myrtle handed Regan her apron as she passed. "You were all excited to not be sleeping in the motel. Is the apartment not comfortable?"

"No. It's great. The bed is stupid-comfortable." Regan tied off the apron and scanned the room. Lucky for her there weren't a lot of customers yet. Her guilt was mildly alleviated that she hadn't left Myrtle in the lurch.

"So?"

"Oh, right. It's just—I've never stayed anywhere alone." From living with her parents as a child, onto her roommate in the dorms her one semester in college, and then right in with Tony, she'd always lived with someone else. "I thought it was just the hotel, but I'm just not used to being alone."

"Everything is much louder and quieter all at once that first time." Myrtle squeezed her shoulder. "I know how it feels."

"I'm sure I'll get used to it eventually. It's just weird." Weird, creepy, scary, whatever one would call it. Either way, Regan had tossed and turned all night. Without any sleep the night before, she feared she'd end up dragging her feet all shift.

"Be a dear and cut those lemons for me, would you?" Myrtle hacked away at a head of lettuce behind the counter. "And how is Clay?"

"What?" Regan stopped with the knife barely through the rind. "Why would you ask me that? I mean, what?"

Myrtle chuckled. "Sorry. Just you two seem awful chummy."

"He's been nice." Regan focused on cutting the lemon. Sure, she found Clay attractive, *I mean what girl wouldn't drool over a tall, dark, and handsome cowboy straight out of a movie. One with brains, and gorgeous gray eyes, and...what the hell are you doing?* Regan's shoulders sagged and she focused all her attention on the lemon in front of her. That lemon was far safer than thoughts of Clay.

Last thing she needed was a man. After Tony, she'd be fine never even being friends with another guy.

"Regan?" Myrtle's hand rested on her shoulder. "What is it, child?"

Myrtle's attentions made Regan aware of the tear on her cheek. Regan hooked her finger and wiped it away with her knuckle to avoid lemon juice anywhere near her eye. She cleared her throat and tried to come up with a good explanation. After everything, it seemed silly to miss Tony, he was the reason she'd left.

"You miss your family?"

"No." Regan closed her eyes, cursing her frank admission. Years ago she'd given up hope of her family caring anymore. They'd disowned her when she'd left college, or rather flunked out. She sighed. "I don't know. My head is a mess."

"Your head? Or your heart?"

"Yes." To both.

"Must have been tough leaving everything."

She hadn't had much to leave, but it still kept her up at night. The effort it had taken to leave had been herculean. "I just don't know if I did the right thing."

"Sometimes the right thing to do is the hardest thing to do." Myrtle tossed the lettuce into a bin, and started in on the carrots. "I've been there a few times in my life."

Regan had little doubt Myrtle meant what she said. "I guess."

"You happy here?"

"Here?" Regan glanced around the small, neat café. Only a few tables were full, but she already knew all their names. Despite being in New York, which she'd heard was full of rude cities and people, this place had a small town feel like where she'd lived in Illinois. "I think so. I don't really know it that well, yet." Why she'd made it conditional, she didn't know. Instinct, maybe. Instinct to keep guarded.

"You know their names?" Myrtle shook her peeler toward the occupied booths.

"Yes."

"Then you know it well enough. Lake Point is a good little town. Once you know the lie-abouts like them, you're in." Myrtle paused to wink before she resumed her attention to the carrots. "I think sometimes you just know in your heart when you're home, and you can relax."

"What if you don't trust your heart?" Though she'd kept her words quiet, Regan could still feel Myrtle's strong gaze on her. Heat flamed her cheeks and she gathered the cut lemons into the bucket. "I should go put these in the cooler."

Regan walked as quick as she could back to the cooler, out of view of Myrtle. She stepped into the cold room with a sigh of relief, letting the cold soak through her shame. If she'd come here to escape, she was doing a terrible job. Her mind just wouldn't let go, or was it her heart?

She honestly didn't know the last time she'd felt free. The simple word 'free' brought up images of the beach when she was a child, before her family had left California. Her brother and she had chased the seagulls into flight, and her dad had stumbled away cursing when another gull pooped on his bald head. If nothing else, the memory helped her find a smile again.

The long breath she released clouded in the cool air of the refrigerator. She watched her own breath curl in a fog that dissipated under the blast of the fans, and her tension dissipated with it. Calmer now, she turned and yanked open the door.

She rubbed away the goosebumps on her way up front, where she found Myrtle chatting with a young woman at the counter. Regan guessed the girl was a few years younger than herself; pretty, with caramel-colored hair and blue eyes.

"There you are. Come here, Regan. I was just talking about you." Myrtle waved her over to the counter. "This here is Veronica Neeley."

"Call me Roni, please." Roni grinned and offered a small wave. "Veronica is so pretentious. I always hated it."

Regan smiled in return. "Hi."

"Roni just got home from her freshman year." Myrtle straightened to wipe down the counter. "She might be a big college girl out in Ohio, but she's from here. I thought she might be able to help you find things to do when you aren't here. You're close enough in age."

Regan bit back the urge to laugh out loud, and noticed Roni hide her own laugh behind her hand. After she'd managed to curb her laughter, Regan nodded. "I suppose we are."

Roni waited until Myrtle excused herself with some excuse about the day's pies before she leaned forward. "Don't think she realizes it sounds like she set us up on a blind date."

"No, pretty sure she's just trying to meddle." Regan shrugged. She adjusted her apron and dropped her order pad into the pocket. Much as Roni's joking observation was true, Regan was sure this girl wouldn't want to hang out.

"She's right, though. I can't give you tips on bars, but I do know a good dance club, if you like that sort of thing." Roni sipped her drink.

"I don't drink anyway. Never liked it." Regan prayed for the distraction of another customer. She'd never been good at making friends, ever; she hadn't had the 'it' factor her brother had that made popularity and friendships so easy for him. "Look, I know Myrtle put you up to this."

"Oh." Roni pursed her lips and swirled her straw in her drink. Her shoulders sagged a little. "I get it. I'm only eighteen."

"What? No, that's not it. I thought you were just suggesting it for Myrtle."

"Problem with a dance club is I don't think Clay would go."

"Probably not—wait, what?"

A slow grin curled Roni's lips. "Sorry. Couldn't resist. I've only been home a couple days, but word of the cowboy's valiant rescue already reached me."

Regan groaned and buried her face in her hands. "Maybe that small town thing isn't as good as it seems."

"Sometimes it really isn't." Roni laughed. She held out her hand. "Why don't we start again, without the awkward blind date set up feel, huh? I'm Veronica, but I prefer Roni."

"Regan." She shook Roni's hand. "Why do you prefer a boy's name?"

"Oh, you start with the hard-hitting questions. Fair enough, I don't like Veronica for two reasons. First, because I was named for a character in comics, and really? Second, I'm a total tomboy and Veronica is way too girly."

"Fair enough." Regan leaned on the counter. "Myrtle said Neeley, as in the Neeley's with the B&B, and where Clay boards his horse?"

"Yup. I love working in the barn with my dad, even though Mom would rather I became a doctor like her, I'm pretty sure it's not going to happen. So what's with you and Clay? Anything? If so, I'm totally jealous. I used to crush on him so hard."

"Nothing." Regan spoke too fast. True or not, answers fast as hers always led to doubt, and she could see the doubt all over Roni's face. Regan sighed, and shrugged. "Okay, so he's cute, but trust me when I say I don't, I can't, ever again, like a guy."

"Turned lesbian or sworn off men?"

"Sworn off men."

"You do realize that's the surest way to find one, don't you?"

"Not this girl."

"Ri-ight."

* * * *

Clay pulled his office door shut. After a crazy busy month in May, he'd had to play a lot of catch up on his paperwork. Lucky for him, he'd had the cursing company of Tag working on his Nova out in the garage until around nine.

Although Clay didn't mind being alone in the quiet when he had work to do, the comic relief of Tag working on his car helped the time go faster. Unfortunately, even with that, it had taken until ten-thirty to finish everything.

At least he was done until payday now. He dropped his hat on his head and strode from the garage, locking the door behind him. Years ago he'd sealed off access to his apartment from inside the garage. He liked to leave the building physically, even if he was just going outside and upstairs. It gave him a sense of leaving work, even if it was just a technicality.

On his way to the stairs, the lights from the diner drew his attention. He wasn't even sure if Regan was working that day, and the diner closed at ten, but he checked anyway.

Inside, Regan leaned on the jukebox. She tapped her lip before she reached out and hit a few buttons. Clay grinned when she started to shake her hips.

Just before he turned away, she spun and began to dance through the restaurant. Clay froze with his hand on the railing, captivated by her movements, and the bright smile she wore.

Somehow she incorporated wiping down tables and booths in her dance. The moves were like those he'd seen on that dance competition show his sister watched whenever she visited. With natural grace, she bent and turned and spun through the room.

When she kicked her leg high and arched back, Clay's mouth went dry. "Damn." Sure, he'd seen the girls on Cadence's favorite show, but never so close, and never someone he knew. His attraction to Regan had just gone through the roof.

She'd dropped to the floor after the move, and that gave Clay a moment to shake the sudden dirty thoughts from his head. He liked her, a lot, but she was skittish as hell and didn't need a horny guy trying to ease his hard-on around. Even if it was true at this point.

Regan reappeared, wiping down a table as if nothing had happened. Clay's disappointment eased when Myrtle came into view. Maybe she'd stopped just because of Myrtle's arrival.

Which meant not only did she not want to be seen, but he would probably come off as some weird stalker dude if he stuck around much longer. Unless—he knew it was unlikely Ivy was still at the studio. This was something she had to see, she'd know if Regan had skill or Clay was just blinded by lust.

Regan stretched across a table to put up some salt and pepper shakers. After she'd peeked over her shoulder, she started to move again. Her hips swayed, and Clay had to forcibly pry his gaze away to let her dance in the peace she wanted.

He closed his eyes and willed away his lust as best as he could. For the time being, he had to think with the right brain. After a deep breath, he pulled his phone out and flipped through the contacts. When he found the one for Ivy's studio, he hesitated.

Hedging his bets, he pocketed his phone and headed for his truck instead of upstairs. What he needed was a beer and some sense knocked into him. Tag had mentioned something about heading to the bar with Mikey, so Clay headed that way.

The short drive wasn't quite enough to cool his head, and finding Tag and Mikey making out in their booth didn't help matters. He slapped the table, and cheered a little when they both jumped. "Get a room."

"We plan to." Tag waved over the waitress and ordered another round of beers for them all.

"You don't look happy." Mikey's brow puckered in concern. She leaned forward. "Is something wrong?"

"No. I'm fine." Clay wiped his hand over his face to try to erase whatever sign of his inner struggle she'd seen. He dropped the hat onto the seat beside him.

"Sure. I believe you." Mikey finished off her beer and set it aside as the waitress placed their fresh bottles on the table. Up until she'd started seeing Tag and helping him out with his car, Clay had seen Mikey more as an acquaintance. Over the past few months she'd become a good friend, one that could spot his lie a mile away. "Spill, Clay."

"Is it the girl?" Tag grunted when Mikey elbowed him. "What?"

"She's older than you, boy. Don't call her 'girl'." She rolled her eyes, but her grin grew. "Oh, is he right? Is it Regan?"

"Doesn't matter, either way." Clay drank a long swig of beer to try to cool the fire in his belly. Of course, it didn't have any effect at all.

"I think we can take that as a yes. I knew you liked her, but you like her, eh?" Tag wagged his brows. "Do I need to pester you as much as you pestered me?"

"No. Regan doesn't need that. From what Myrtle was saying, she's skittish." Mikey shook her head. "Pick on Clay all you want in private, but leave her alone."

"Gee, thanks," Clay muttered dryly.

"So what's her story? I mean other than the lemon she rode in on." Tag spun his bottle on the table. "Auntie M said she's from Illinois?"

"Supposedly. I don't know much about her." Clay tapped his thumb against the label. "She's a self-proclaimed geek, has a brother she doesn't talk to, and does not like to talk about her past at all."

"I—"

"And she's a hell of a dancer," Clay continued without even thinking. When he lifted his head, Mikey looked more amused than annoyed he'd interrupted her.

"She what?" Mikey leaned forward. "How did you learn this?"

"By accident." Clay sank back in the seat, guilt rising again. "I didn't mean to watch."

"What happened?" Mikey smacked Tag to stop his snickering.

"I just went out to go upstairs after I was done with work and saw her in the diner. She started dancing, and I couldn't stop watching for a minute. She was…" Clay took another swig of beer to erase the renewed dryness of his mouth. Picturing the scene again wasn't helping him cool off at all. "Cadence makes me watch that dance show, and she was as good as them. Better."

"You mean that one with the Hollywood stars?" Tag wrinkled his nose. "Ugh."

"No. The other one." Clay chuckled. "Cadey says they're all amateurs."

"Oh, Dance For Your Life." Mikey nodded. "I watched that after the divorce when all I did was lie around in a depression. Those kids were good. She really danced like that?"

"I almost called Ivy, then figured it was none of my business. She obviously didn't want to be seen, she stopped when Myrtle came in the room." Clay shook his head. "I can't get that out of my head. It's not right, I don't even know her that well. Much as I'd like to."

Tag and Mikey glanced at each other, and Clay immediately regretted the admittance. In the end, it was Tag that spoke. "So get to know her. We've got that party at the shore this weekend. Have her come. It's neutral, and maybe you can get more out of her."

"Maybe." Clay peeled the label off the bottle. "I guess there's no harm in asking."

"Just don't present it like a date," Mikey cautioned. "If she's as skittish as you and Myrtle say, make sure you say it's a party and you're inviting her in general. Offer to drive her since she doesn't have a car, but do not say 'go with me'."

"Okay."

"I'm serious."

"Yes ma'am."

Chapter Four

Clay propped his arms on his knees, an untouched lemonade in one hand. Soon as they'd arrived, Regan had been dragged off by Roni. With that went Clay's plan to get to know Regan any better.

The party was supposed to go most of the day, but Clay had never been much of a 'beach' guy. He wore jeans in the summer, and rarely went swimming. Regan, however, had apparently taken the beach party idea to heart, and wore a simple bathing suit with shorts. She'd tossed her sandals and gotten caught up in a volleyball game.

For his part, Clay sat on a picnic bench under the cool shade of a tree. He'd pondered a beer, but when Regan had rejected his offer of a beer, he'd settled for lemonade.

"You do know this is a party, right?" Eve Ellery, Mikey's best friend and manager of the antique shop in town, Past Over, hopped onto the table next to him. "I'm surprised so many of the younger ones showed up. I'm guessing that's Tag's doing. That boy could charm the bark off of a tree."

Clay snorted. "Yeah, I know. You like the jail bait."

Delicate pink tinted Eve's cheeks, but she shrugged. "It's always nice to have eye candy around. Cowboys aren't so bad either, you know."

"And yet, I think neither are what you like." Clay glanced sideways at her. "Where's Jake?"

The pink deepened to red and she sighed. "Business trip. As usual. Not sure how the two are related. Just hush, all right? Tell me where she is. I haven't had a chance to meet her yet."

"Mikey's got a big mouth."

"Only with me. Now where is she?"

He jerked his chin toward the volleyball game. "Purple suit."

"Nice. She's cute." Eve leaned back on the table top. "Looks like she's a beach bunny. That means you're going to have to bathing-suit up and get out of those boots if you want to talk to her, you know."

"I'm not a beach guy."

"And I'm not a beach girl, I mean really, me and bathing suits are not friends."

"Stop that talk. You're gorgeous." Clay nudged her and frowned. One thing he never understood was Eve's obsession with beating people to the punch.

"Says the man drooling over the model-figure new girl." She winked, and her smile was bright. Unlike her previous statement, her voice carried no sadness. "Anyway, even I managed to get into some summer clothes. You should do the same, or else you'll remain here pouting under a tree until we light up the grills and you have something to do."

"I'm not pouting."

"Then take off your pants and boots and get out in the sun, goober."

"Goober? Really? What are we, five?"

"On a good day." Eve pushed to her feet and set her hands on her hips. "Don't make me get Mikey and Deanna. We'll gang up on you in a heartbeat. You're supposed to be having fun, after all. Grab a beer, go play badminton or horseshoes, and stop being anti-social."

"Wow, you and Mikey can be real bossy when you want to be." Clay ducked away from her swatting hands. "Hey, hey, hey!"

"Punk." Eve's laughter joined his and she shoved him.

He snatched her around the waist and tossed her over his shoulder. Her shriek pierced his ear drum, but he laughed. During her struggle, he held her firm so she wouldn't fall. "Now what are you gonna do?"

"Put me down." She smacked his back. "You'll break your back liftng me."

"You kidding? You're light as a feather." A lifetime of tossing hay and raising horses made his statement true as could be. "Now are you gonna stop picking on me?"

"Never." She started to pound on his back. "Nice as your ass is, and as much as I'm enjoying the view, I'd like down now."

"Promise."

"No."

"I'll throw you in the lake."

"Don't you dare, Clayton Ryley!"

By that point, they'd drawn some attention, including that of Regan. Clay thought he was imagining the flush that filled her cheeks and the disappointment puckering her brow. He had to be, because she turned away a second later.

Eve squirmed harder, drawing his full attention back to her so he made sure he didn't accidentally drop her. "Clay!"

"Promise." He toed off his boots and kicked them aside.

"Please put me down. I'm wearing a white shirt. Really, Clay. I'm not joking."

"Me either." He started toward the water, the sand squishing beneath his toes before she started to squirm again. "Promise and I'll let you down."

"I won't cave to blackmail."

"Suit yourself." He picked up a little speed, knowing he'd regret it when he'd have to take his wet jeans off later, but not caring. At the edge of the water, Eve shrieked, and he paused. "Are you going to promise?"

She struggled against his hold again. Her hands braced on his back, but even after another hard shove, she was still stuck. "Damn you, Clay."

"Just promise."

"No."

"All right." He waded into the water. The water was cold enough to be a shock to the system. He shook it off and moved deeper until he stopped noticing the cold. When he got almost waist deep, he heard her laughter. "Eve?"

"I knew I'd get you in the water!"

"You little—" When he flipped her back over his shoulder and she went under with a splash.

She jumped up to her feet, flipping her soaked blond hair back. Her laughter rang out even as she wiped the water from her features. "DeeDee owes me twenty bucks."

"You snot!" Clay laughed and gave her a half-hearted shove.

Eve pushed him back hard enough to make him stumble into the water. "Now you've had your soak—go get into your suit, you jerk. Regan is watching us all sad and forlorn. I think she wants some of your attention."

"She's not." He got to his feet and peeled off his shirt.

"Well if she wasn't, she sure is now." Eve turned him around and pushed him toward shore. "Get out of those jeans and give her something to drool over."

Clay grunted. Even from where they were he could see she had a point. Regan's attention was on him now. She was sipping her water bottle at the edge of the volleyball court, but was watching them, not the game. He pushed Eve back toward the group. "Okay, you go get your twenty bucks. And thanks."

"Don't mention it. Next time don't play so shy…you're a good guy. Irresistible to women as Tag once you turn on that good ol' boy southern charm." She winked and headed toward where Ivy, Mikey, and Deanna were catching some rays.

On his way to the truck, he took a detour by the volleyball court. He smiled, trying to keep it in place when Regan ducked her head. "Having fun?"

"Yeah." Regan fiddled with her water bottle cap. "What was that about?"

"Eve was yelling at me for sitting around in jeans." Clay held up his soaked shirt and wrung it out, splashing water on both their feet. "I fell into her trap and let her get me in the water, thinking I was the one pulling a fast one on her."

She yelped and jumped back. "That water's not the warmest."

"Not really." He chuckled. "But now I have to get my suit on. Want to take a walk once I'm ready? We got a while before they light the grills."

"Um, sure." She worried her lip between her teeth, her eyes darting over toward where Eve and the others were. "If you want."

"I do. Give me five minutes."

* * * *

Regan gulped down her water while she waited. *Get a grip on yourself.* She dropped the water bottle in a nearby trash can, unable to stop herself from looking toward Clay's truck. He'd set his hat on top of the cab and stood behind the door fighting with his soaked jeans.

Wonder if he's got his suit underneath that or— She gasped at her own thoughts and turned away. The jealousy that had sparked when she'd seen him goofing around with the blond woman made no sense. Then again, it made perfect sense.

That woman had curves—curves Regan had never been able to attain. No matter that she ate like a pig, she'd still had a teacher ask her in front of an entire class of kids once if she was anorexic. 'Eat a pork chop' her friend had teased. Senior year she'd finally sprouted boobs, but she'd still kill for curves like the blond.

That's what men liked. Tony told her time and again she was too skinny. 'The anorexic jokes are old. Would you eat already'?

Regan closed her eyes against the memory and took a deep breath. Now was not the time to let in thoughts like that. She'd actually been having a good time for a change. Good times never lasted, though.

"Sorry about that." Clay's warm hand rested on her shoulder, startling her back to reality. "I grabbed a couple more waters. It's hot out today."

"Thanks." Regan reached for the water, her fingers brushed his when she grabbed it. When his hand lingered for a moment, her heart jumped, but then he pulled back as fast. She fell into step next to him as they headed down the beach away from the crowd.

In the lingering silence, she wondered why he'd invited her to walk. Clearly this wasn't a date, he'd only offered to drive, and she would have turned down a date. Or would she?

She groaned. The sooner her heart and head got themselves straight, the better off she'd be. When Clay's gaze lingered on her, she realized she'd groaned out loud. Rather than let him confront that, she jumped to speak first, "Why were you sitting in jeans?"

"I've never been a beach person. I like open fields, mountains, farms, horses. I've never been much for the beach or water. I learned to swim because my mom made us all learn."

"Really? I love the water. We used to go to the beach all the time when we lived in California. I was such a water baby."

"Do you miss it?"

"California?" She shrugged at his nod. "I haven't been back in so long. I try not to think about it too much."

"What about your family?"

She slowed her pace, buying time by popping open her water. Talking about her family was more painful than anything. They'd abandoned her—and now she'd abandoned everything. She had to escape answering the question. "What about you? I know you miss your family, do you miss South Carolina?"

His smile faltered and his features pinched in disappointment. After a moment, he shook his head and looked off across the lake. "Sometimes more than others. I got plenty to love right here. I've been in New York for eight years now. I know Lake Point nearly as well as I did Camden."

"I imagine the small town feel helped."

"It's part of why I stayed." He glanced toward the group down the beach. "Good friends that are like family make all the difference."

She spotted a good skipping stone and bent to scoop it up. "Maybe we should avoid such depressing topics. We might get yelled at for not enjoying the party." Plus, if they avoided touchy topics, she wouldn't feel pressured to reveal any more of her past.

"You want to talk about cars?"

"Ooooh, nope." Regan laughed and skipped her stone across the surface of the lake. "I wouldn't know a carburetor from a radiator. As far as models of cars, I know what a few of them are, otherwise I'm clueless."

"Horses."

"I keep meaning to get out to the Neeley's. Roni promised a tour. Unfortunately, I've forgotten much of what

I learned when I was younger. I'd be happy to listen, but I'd be clueless to contribute to the conversation."

"You're making this difficult." He quirked a brow.

"You're at two strikes." She was relieved to find him smiling. For some reason his disappointment bothered her. "You know what they say about three strikes."

"I'd like to see you do better."

"Nope, not yet. You are only at two strikes."

"Cookies!"

The desperation in his voice almost made her snort and giggle, but she sucked her lips between her teeth to try to stop it. When he turned toward her, she turned away and lifted her shoulders in a dramatic sigh. "I guess there's just nothing for us to talk about."

"Star Trek."

"Too late. It was your third try." She giggled and turned toward him. "It was a good one, too. I've got a killer sweet tooth, although how to carry on a conversation about cookies?"

The tension in his features drained away and a sexy grin formed.

Sexy? What are you doing to yourself?

"Do you like yours crunchy or soft?"

"I do hope you're talking about cookies." Her cheeks grew tight from her grin as red seeped into his cheeks. "Oh, did I forget to mention that my mind is often in the gutter?"

He chuckled and shook his head. "You hadn't. I guess I'll have to watch what I say."

"Won't work."

"Thanks for the warning."

"Happy to help." She dropped to the sand and waited for him to join her. "As far as cookies go, I like the classic ooey, gooey chocolate chip. I don't like them crunchy. I'm also a fan of snickerdoodles and peanut butter blossoms. But nothing with raisins. Ick."

He pursed his lips. "You don't like raisins?"

"Nope."

"Well there you go."

"There you go?" This could go either way. "Are you saying raisins are a deal breaker?"

"They are."

She caught the twitch of his lip, and grinned. If he wanted to tease her back, she'd probably earned it, but she'd be happy to join in. "So now we can't be friends?"

"Just the opposite. I despise raisins. Onions too."

"Really? I hate onions." She touched his arm. "Please tell me you aren't kidding. I never find anyone that hates them as much as I do."

"I really do." He leaned in close. "I tell restaurants I'm allergic to them to get them to keep from 'accidentally' putting them in my dish."

"I never thought of that. That's awesome! I have to try it."

His grin grew even bigger. "Well there you go. I guess we have to be friends."

Her stomach did a little flutter unlike she'd felt in years, and for a moment she couldn't form words. She wanted him to kiss her, so much. With a gasp, she ducked her head. There was no way he wanted the same, and she was stupid to want it.

"Regan?" His warm hand settled on her shoulder.

"I don't know." She tried to keep her tone light. "What about tomatoes?"

"I'll eat them, but I'm not a big fan."

"I suppose that's acceptable." She turned back toward him, surprised to find him still so close she almost did kiss him. "Oh."

"Sorry."

"You don't look sorry." She backed off a few inches in an attempt to curb her own desire to kiss him. Truth be told, it didn't help at all. *He doesn't want to kiss you, you fool.*

He shrugged and brushed the sand from his hands. "I'm not."

Her heart hammered in her chest when he leaned closer again.

A few inches away, he stopped and met her gaze. "Favorite Star Trek character?"

"All of the series, or just one?"

"All of them."

She swore he was moving closer, but that didn't happen to her. Not with more attractive women everywhere. Instinct made her duck her head away. "I can't pick."

"Good answer."

"Really?" She turned back and he was close enough to kiss again. "Clay?"

"Sorry."

"No. You're not"

His gaze flickered away from her lips to meet her eyes. "Is that okay?"

"What?" She backed off more in surprise than anything. Was he asking her permission? Men didn't do that.

"Are you all right?" He touched her cheek. "You look pale."

"I…"

"I'm sorry. I'll back off."

"No!" She clamped her hands over her mouth in surprise at how fast the protest came out. Slowly, she peeled them away, trying to ignore the embarrassment and nerves twisting her stomach into knots. "I didn't say that. I just…I'm confused."

"About what?" He tilted his head. "You've been kissed before, right?"

"Yes." She shook her head. "You want to kiss me?"

"Have for a while. Didn't want to scare you off like I seem to be doing."

"No one ever wants to kiss me. Not even…" She closed her eyes against the rush of emotions. When his finger touched her cheek and wiped away a tear, she jerked in surprise.

"I'd sound like a total creep if I said I wanted to the night I met you, wouldn't I?"

"No. It would be a first, though."

"I doubt that."

She looked down at the sand, fiddling with a seashell.

"Regan." He tucked a finger under her chin. "May I?"

"What's your favorite Star Trek character?"

"All of them."

"Then yes."

His warm chuckle filled the air moments before his lips touched hers. The soft strength of his kiss was just how she'd imagined.

She sighed, relaxing into the kiss as he slowly coaxed it deeper. Just as his tongue brushed the seam of her lips, a gull shrieked nearby and startled them both. She giggled as the bird waddled toward them, shrieked again and took off. "I guess we offended him."

"Apparently so." His laughter joined hers. "Maybe we should head back, I can smell the charcoal already."

"Oh." Disappointment tugged her previous excitement away.

"Maybe later we can try again where we won't be offending the local wildlife."

"I'd like that."

Chapter Five

Regan ripped her brush through her hair for the tenth time that morning. The braid she kept trying to put in would not fall into place. She glared at her reflection. "You're an idiot. What were you thinking?"

Never in her whole life had a man as attractive as Clay given her a second glance. All of her crushes had been from a distance, and none of them could be bothered to give her the time of day. She just wasn't that attractive or popular.

She turned away from the mirror to try to get the braid in blind. When Clay had removed his shirt, she'd lost her good sense. The man had strong broad shoulders, and arms with just the right amount of muscle to make her literally swoon if she wasn't too proud.

Clay Ryley was like a page out of her teenage fantasies—all romantic cowboy, strong muscles and that smile—exactly the sort of man that wouldn't ever really want her.

"They're probably all laughing at you. You're just a cruel, stupid joke to them. You're so freaking stupid." She dropped her painfully tight grasp on her hair and let her arms hang at her sides. Tingles crept along her skin as the blood returned to her arms.

Her alarm went off in the next room, startling her back to the present. "Shit. I'm going to be late." She ran to slam her hand on the clock to turn it off, and grabbed her apron.

The second she was out the door, she swept her hair up into a ponytail and prayed it would hold for her shift. She skidded to a stop outside The Diner when she spotted Clay inside. *Crap. Is he here to laugh in my face?*

She swallowed against the nerves, after all she had to go to work. Maybe she could get by without talking to him, or anyone, beyond what was necessary for her job. Or maybe she was just a fool on all counts. Yes, that was probably it.

After a bracing breath, she opened the door and rushed to the counter. She kept her head down, afraid to see Clay's reaction to her arrival as she tied on her apron.

"Regan." Clay appeared at the edge of her vision, hovering against the counter. "I was going to call, but then I remembered you don't have a phone yet."

"Oh, I did get a phone." She fiddled with the edge of counter, her nail tracing long the seam of the Formica. "I thought you knew."

"No. You'll have to give me your number."

She pinched her lip between her teeth, hoping the pain would erase the burgeoning hope his mere presence had sparked. "I guess. If you want it, I mean."

"Hey." He tapped the back of her hand with his finger. When she still didn't look up, he leaned on the counter to meet her gaze. "I didn't get a chance to ask you last night if you wanted to go out. If you have a lunch or dinner free this week, that is."

"I…" She met his gaze and searched for signs of deception or the cruel glee she was so used to. Nothing but his earnest gaze fixed on her as it had been the day before. "Really?"

His brows rose and he straightened. "Of course. Do you think I'd joke about that?"

"I just—I guess—I don't know. Excuse me." She turned and darted into the kitchen, all the way back to the cooler. Inside, she let the cold air chill her embarrassment as best as it could. Why did she have to be such a socially awkward, stupid fool all the time?

The door opened with a suctioning pop, and the cold air swirled the frozen condensation around before settling. Clay stepped into the room and let the door close behind him. "If you like the cold so much, you picked the right place to live."

"I didn't pick it, my car did." She groaned and pinched the bridge of her nose. "I'm sorry. I'm a mess."

"All I did was ask you on a date. I'm sorry if it upset you."

"It didn't. I'm just not used to it." She rubbed the back of her neck. "Guys like you don't talk to girls like me, much less kiss them and ask them on dates."

"Guys…like me?"

"Yeah. You know. You're—" She sucked her lips between her teeth before the word *hot* escaped from her lips.

An amused smile rose on his features. "I'm what?"

"Nice?" Even she didn't believe herself with that cracking tone, so it was no surprise when he snorted. "Are you going to give me an out?"

"Not a chance."

She wondered if she was fast or wily enough to get around him and out the door before she had to answer. While he held his silent stance, she fiddled with her apron ties. Finally she managed to whisper, "You're hot."

When he started to chuckle, she turned away and gripped her stomach. Here it came, just like always. She really was a fool.

* * * *

At first, Clay wasn't sure he heard her correctly, and then he just couldn't believe she'd make such a comment and mean it. He chuckled, thinking for sure she was kidding. As gorgeous as she was, she couldn't doubt someone like him could like her.

She turned away, and a sniffle carried over his laughter. Even from behind he could see her wiping at tears.

His laughter died on his lips and he stepped closer. The moment he did, her shoulders tensed. Concern replaced his amusement. "I'm not laughing at you. I thought you were kidding."

"It's okay." She wiped the corners of her eyes and turned toward him, keeping her gaze lowered. "I get it."

"Get what?"

"I've never had that thing that made people popular and liked. It's not the first time I've been the brunt of some joke."

His body went numb, but not from the cold of the freezer. When she moved to get around him, he stepped into her path. "Wait just a minute. That isn't me. I wouldn't do that to anyone, and I sure as hell wouldn't do such a thing to you."

"Can we stop this now? Please?"

"Not until you look me in the eye."

She wrung her hands, her gaze not wavering from the door. "I'm late for work. You'll get me in trouble with Myrtle. This job is all I've got."

"No it's not, and Myrtle will be fine."

She released a breath that fogged and condensed in the cold air before she lifted her hands to cover her face.

Every instinct told him to comfort her, but he worried she'd react poorly to that as well. He stepped closer, and when she took a half step back, he set his hands on her shoulders to hold her in place. "Regan."

"Just go. You're making it worse."

"Making what worse? I don't even know exactly what's going on, except that someone I care about is upset." At her sob, he pulled her close against him. He held her shivering body, and kissed the top of her head. "Did you think that kiss was a joke?"

Every inch of her grew tense in his arms. Silence lingered before she finally answered his question with a stiff nod.

"I like you, for real. I think you're beautiful."

She scoffed and shook her head again.

"I think you're beautiful. I'm just getting to know you, but you seem real smart. Sweet. Sarcastic. Funny. And as scared as a cat at the dog pound."

"I—what?" She sniffed and finally met his eyes. Confusion, and finally a bit of amusement lingered in her features.

He grinned. "You heard me."

A brief smile lifted her lips before she ripped her gaze away and took a step back. "Anyway. Who said I was scared?"

"What else would you call it?" He kept his hand on her arms so she couldn't pull all the way away. If she did, he wasn't sure he'd ever be able to convince her that he really did like her.

"I don't know."

"Will you look at me now?"

She shuffled her feet and rubbed her forearms. After a few minutes, her gaze slowly lifted. The shimmering hint of tears lingered in her eyes.

"I liked kissing you yesterday. I do want to take you out." Clay kept his gaze level, hoping she could see how much he meant every word. "Unless you don't want to."

Her lip trembled, and her cheeks darkened. "I do. I just can't believe you do."

"Believe it. When are you free?"

"If I'm fired, right now."

He tapped her nose and shook his head. "Myrtle's not going to fire you. Don't be so negative. When are you free?"

"I'm off on Tuesday."

"Lunch? Dinner?"

"All day." She took a deep breath and seemed to steady herself. "I have every Tuesday off. I was going to get a library card, and visit the rescue shelter to look for a cat."

"Then we'll plan for dinner on Tuesday."

"Dinner." She nodded. After a moment, she lifted her chin again. "Nowhere fancy, I only have jeans."

"Works for me. I like casual." He rubbed her arms when she shivered. "Let's get out of here before we freeze to death."

"Too late." She pushed open the door and hopped out of the cooler. Fists clenched at her sides, she shuddered. "Brr."

He rubbed his own arms, chuckling. "You have to pick a warmer hiding place."

"The cold cools me down. I don't usually stay in there that long." She sighed. "I should get to work."

Clay hopped into step beside her. "A cat?"

"Turns out, I don't like being by myself. I'd get a dog, but with my hours that didn't seem fair." She was still rubbing her arms when they stepped out of the kitchen. "I always liked cats, but my mom was allergic. Now I can get one."

"Makes sense."

Myrtle stepped behind the counter, a bright grin as she looked between them. "Well, there you are. Thought I'd lost you both."

"I'm so sorry." Regan's voice squeaked in her panic. "It won't happen again."

"Oh, don't you worry, none. We're not that busy yet, and I'm the one that sent Clay here after you. You okay?" Myrtle shoved an order ticket in the carousel and spun it to the back. "You need some more time?"

"No. I'm fine." Regan's gaze darted toward Clay before she looked down. "But I should get to work."

Clay didn't want to let her go that easy, but she needed to work. He squeezed her shoulder. "I'll see you Tuesday, if not sooner."

"Right. See you then." She darted away, but not before he saw her smile.

Myrtle gave him a stern look. "Well?"

"I don't rightly know what freaked her out so bad. She thought I was playing a cruel joke on her by kissing her yesterday or something." Clay kept his tone low. The diner wasn't that big, after all. "But I think I got her calmed down. We're going out for dinner Tuesday."

"Tread lightly, boy. That girl'd sooner run than be happy." Myrtle patted his arm. "Now sit down, I'll feed you before you go for your ride. Need a basket?"

"Nah. Not going to be out long today. I promised Tag and Mikey I'd let them in the shop today. They're determined to get that Nova going."

"I tried to tell Tag that beast is a lost cause." Mytrle set a plate of fries in front of him.

"Mikey's more stubborn than he is about it. She swears it can be done." He shoved a fry in his mouth. Even if he'd tried, he wouldn't have been able to stop tracking Regan as she walked behind the counter. Despite her clear trepidation and damage, something about her drew him in.

"I noticed that. She's making him work on it harder than he was." Myrtle's voice drew him back to the conversation. "Maybe that means he will actually get it done."

"I know better than to argue with a stubborn woman, and if she says they can get it done, they will." He grinned and pulled his plate of fries closer. "Then again, you say it can't, so which stubborn woman should I believe?"

"Oh you, hush up. Eat your fries and get out of my hair."

"Yes ma'am."

* * * *

Regan sat at the counter, eying the booth in the corner. Her shift had ended twenty minutes before, and that booth had been her last table to be served. Immediately after her shift, she'd ordered food and sat at the counter to eat. Already she'd eaten her salad and half of her burger, but the table she'd waited on earlier hadn't left yet. She preferred to have every bit of her tips before she went home.

She trusted Myrtle completely, and didn't worry too much about her coworkers. It was just her preference not to leave without the cash in hand. Of course, her last table of the day had to be squatters when all she wanted to do was head home and try to get her head on straight.

She was still in shock over Clay's visit earlier that day. How could he want to take her out on a date? For that matter, why had she said yes?

Sure, she liked him. A girl would have to be flat out nuts not to, but a date? She hadn't been on a date in years. High school was the last time she could remember going on an honest to goodness date.

The bell on the door jingled and Roni entered. Instantly, the girl found Regan and gave her a bright smile. Regan had a sinking feeling that word had already gotten out about Tuesday.

Soon as she sat down, Roni confirmed Regan's worries. "Glad you're still here, is it true? You and Clay are going out?"

"Did someone take out a billboard?" Regan groaned and dropped her head into her hand.

"Small town. Word gets around fast. Clay told Tag, of course. Tag told Michaela, who told Eve, and so on."

"I don't see why it's so darn interesting."

"Clay hardly ever dates, that's how. Plenty of girls in town have tried. He's a hell of a catch. I'm too young, didn't stop me from crushing crazy on him when he came by the ranch."

Regan sighed. At least most of the talk was more about him than her. She pushed away her plate. "I was crazy to say yes."

"No. You'd be crazy if you'd said no." Roni leaned closer. "You know that, right?"

"I don't date. I haven't in years. I don't know how to act. What to do." Regan twirled her knife on the napkin.

"That's easy. You go, relax and have a great time." Roni grinned. "Then let me live vicariously through you with stories of how great it was."

Regan laughed. "You just want stories, huh?"

"The juicier the better."

"I doubt you'll get them this time. We're not even going anywhere fancy. All I've got is jeans and t-shirts."

"That's easily fixable. Come check out my wardrobe."

"No. I'm good." Regan held up her hands and shook her head. "This is me. If he's not going to like me, then he won't like me because I'm my usual dorky self."

"Please. You're hot."

"Ri-ight. I'm also slated to be the next woman in space."

Roni snorted. "Then let's at least raid your closet and come up with the best outfit."

"It's two days away, Roni." Regan didn't want to admit how embarrassingly bare her closet was. She'd left Illinois with a suitcase of all purpose, every day clothes. Even in the few weeks she'd been in Lake Point she hadn't bothered with anything else. The idea of having to only pack one suitcase stayed as appealing as it had the day she'd left home.

"Exactly, and if you don't have anything suitable we are going shopping."

"No, we aren't."

"Yes we are. Either at the mall, my closet, or Sharon's resale shop. Tuesday afternoon."

"I'm going to the shelter Tuesday."

"Perfect. It's right near my place. We can start your shopping there."

Regan dropped her head to the counter. "You aren't going to let me be, are you?"

"Nope." Roni grabbed her arm and gave it a tug. "Let's go."

"Fine. But I'm not shopping."

"Only if you happen to have a drop dead gorgeous shirt in her closet."

She didn't. Regan knew it. "Fine."

"Atta girl."

Chapter Six

Clay pulled his truck into Regan's driveway and turned off the ignition. Nerves were getting the best of him. Between two crazy days at work, and his sister calling the night before and taking three hours to say she was coming to Rochester on an unexpected visit, he hadn't been able to check and see how Regan was feeling.

After Sunday at The Diner when she'd been so stressed out over their kiss, he wondered what he'd be walking into this time. As he stepped out of the truck, he knew he was being watched. Up on the porch he found Mrs. Bell watching him from her perch.

He offered a wave and a smile. "Evening, Mrs. Bell."

"Hello Clay." Mrs. Bell nodded in return. "Wasn't expecting you by tonight."

"Came to see Regan. Always happy to see you too, though." He tapped the edge of his hat, and strode to Regan's door. In a way, he was glad Regan ended up in Mrs. Bell's apartment. The woman missed nothing, and guarded her own like nobody's business.

There wasn't a night you couldn't drive by her home and see her on her porch, waving to people she knew, and eying with suspicion those she didn't. Protective as he felt about Regan just based on what he'd seen of her worries and self-esteem issues, he was glad she'd have someone looking out for her.

Even if it was nosy Mrs. Bell.

Clay blew out a short breath and rubbed his hands together to clear away his nerves. After he felt more secure, he knocked.

"Just a minute! No, Uno," Regan's muffled voice carried exasperation. "Come here, you silly thing."

"Uno?" Clay strained to hear more, but all he heard was a door close and her footsteps. He jumped back when she turned the knob.

"Hey." The smile she offered took his breath away. "Sorry about that."

Clay could only shake his head, unable to find words for a minute. Her dark brown hair flowed down over her shoulders. She'd kept her promise to wear jeans, but they were sexy, tight jeans that hugged every curve.

Her bright green shirt draped across her body, not revealing too much, yet came off as the sexiest thing he'd seen in years. For the first time since they'd met, she wore a touch of makeup, but managed to keep it simple. However, the longer he stared, the more her smile faded.

He managed to snap out of it and shook his head. "Right. Sorry. Hi. Hey. Sorry. Damn, you look amazing."

Regan's mouth opened and closed several times, red hues coloring her cheeks. After a moment, she ducked her head. As she did, movement behind her caught Clay's eye.

A small cat sat in the middle of the hallway. All white with orange tabby patches on her side nose and one ear—the only ear he could see. The cat yawned and began to clean its face. He blinked a few times. "Uh, does that cat have only one ear?"

"That, what? Oh crap. Uno. How did you get out?" Regan's embarrassment seemed to race away with her as she darted toward the cat. She scooped it up and held it close, then cursed under her breath. "And now I've got your fur all over me again."

He chuckled and followed her down the hall. "Uno?"

"I figured one ear and all. Is it corny? The shelter had her named Mimsy and, I cannot in good conscious, call any animal Mimsy."

"I like it." Clay scratched the cat's forehead.

"I don't know how she got out of my room. I closed the door before I came to answer the door. I—oh, I mean, oh hell." Flustered again, she turned and shoved open the door.

"Regan, relax." He followed her into the room, a combination bedroom and living room. He'd known the place was furnished by Mrs. Bell, and the older furniture proved it. Regan had added a few personal touches, but for the most part, it was still devoid of a lived in feeling.

"Sorry. I'm ridiculously nervous." She scratched the cat under its chin, eliciting a deep, rumbling purr.

"Okay. Why don't you tell me about Uno?"

"Well, I told you I was going to the shelter today." She turned her attention to the cat, and her shoulders immediately relaxed. The cat sniffed her nose and then gave it a lick. Regan smiled in response. "They had about a dozen cats, but the moment I saw this little girl, I was hooked."

"I haven't seen a one-eared cat before, and I lived on a farm with barn cats."

"Me either, but I like that she's a little broken. That means she's like me."

The honesty of the statement cut through the room and leveled everything out. Clay worried she'd respond to her admission with more nerves if he dug any deeper, and scrambled for something to say that was safe. "So she's an escape artist, too?"

"Yes." Her smile turned sardonic. "I closed her in here when I went to take my shower, and stepped out to find her in the bathroom. Just now, I closed her in here again only for you to spot her in the hall."

"There must be some way she's getting out."

"Or I'm just terribly unobservant and she sneaks by me when I'm closing the door." Regan shrugged. "As long as she doesn't get out of the apartment and outside, I'll be happy."

"Seems to me once a cat knows where its bread is buttered it doesn't go too far."

"I hope so." She kissed the cat's forehead, and set her on the couch. "So…"

"Are you ready?"

She brushed at the cat hair on her shirt. "Ready as I can be, I guess. I forgot about the downfall to having a pet with fur. I'll never get this out."

He chuckled and held out his hand. "I don't mind. Why don't we head on out. I don't want us to be late."

"Where are we going?" She took his hand and let him lead her from the room. With one more glance at Uno, she closed the door to the room.

"Nope. It's a surprise." He grinned at her gasped protest. "Sorry, but you'll just have to wait and see."

"I don't handle surprises well." She locked the door behind her and followed him to the truck. "You can't just tell me?"

"Sort of ruins the whole surprise aspect, don't you think?"

Her lower lip puffed out in a pout. "I guess."

"Can you trust me?"

"I can try."

* * * *

Regan didn't know whether to be creeped out or excited. After he'd driven her to the edge of downtown Lake Point, Clay had pulled over and asked her to put on a blindfold. When he'd told her he wanted to keep it a surprise until the last possible second, she'd still hesitated. The pout he gave was so pitiful she'd finally caved and put on the blindfold.

From the second it was on, he held her hand and kept up a stream of conversation as if to assure her he wasn't a serial killer like her worst fears, and frequent true-crime show viewing had her thinking. She cleared her throat. "You do know this could be considered really super creepy, right?"

"I know. Sorry. Didn't fully think it out, I just really wanted to surprise you." He gave her hand a gentle squeeze. "But we're almost there. And I, uh…"

Her stomach did a little flip flop at his unease. "What?"

"Well, I was going to ask you to plug your ears."

"Really?" The laughter that she managed to force out sounded more like a nervous titter. She cleared her throat and tried to grin again. "So will I get to be on my favorite show in the next couple of years?"

"Your favorite show?"

"Deadly Encounters."

"Your favorite show is a true crime show?" His chuckle was hesitant, apprehensive. "Then this was a bigger mistake than normal. I'm really not trying to freak you out. Promise. It'll be worth it. I hope."

"Hey, getting on my favorite show isn't so bad." She grinned, then realized it probably made her look crazy and backed it off. "It would give me five seconds of fame, anyway."

"Crappy way to get fame – to be dead, don't you think?"

"Eh." She shrugged. In the past six years she'd spent some time imagining if death would be better than life, which was so insanely hard. The way his hold on her hand tightened brought her back to reality. She tried to brush off her morose thoughts with a laugh. "Hey, if you have to die, might as well get something from it."

He didn't respond aloud, just rubbed her hand. Somehow, she figured he didn't buy her joking excuse of an answer. Hell, she didn't buy it. After another minute, the truck slowed. "Wait here a sec."

"I...okay." She folded her hands in her lap and did her best not to twiddle her thumbs. A short way off she could hear Clay talking to someone, but the rumble of the truck muted anything they said. When the door creaked open again, she cleared her throat. "Clay?"

"Yup. It's me again. Just another few minutes and we'll be set for you to take off the blindfold. Sorry I freaked you out so bad. I really hope this is worth it." Again, he sounded more nervous than she felt.

She reached out to console him, and her hand landed on his strong bicep. The tense muscles jumped under her touch, and she—not unhappily—wrapped her hand around them. "Hey. I told you I would try to trust you. I'm not all that scared right now. I'm mostly teasing."

"It's the 'mostly' word that has me worried." His warm hand settled on hers. "I just hope it's worth all this."

"I hope so too." To be honest, she couldn't believe he was going through so much trouble to surprise her. "You know what?"

"Hold that thought." The truck slowed again, and she heard him set it in park and turn it off. His door opened and then slammed.

She tensed in the sudden silence, and heard his footsteps crunching across gravel. *Okay, so that's a little creepy.* When her door opened, she jumped with a small yelp.

"Here we are. Let me help you to the best spot to see where we are, then you can take that stupid blindfold off." When his hand settled on her arm and he helped her out, she heard other voices. If they were in public, he probably wasn't a serial killer. Or at least not a very good one.

She relaxed at this realization. "Well, we're in public, so you're less likely to be a crazy psycho murderer now, right?"

"Glad you think so. Now hold on, right here." He turned her partway around and then removed his hands from her shoulders. She heard another door latch, and then a thump.

Then his warmth was right in front of her, his hands set gently on her hips. "I need to lift you."

"Oh." When he stepped close enough that their bodies touched, she might have let him do anything. Clear thought flew from her head and she nodded without argument. In the back of her mind, she registered his quiet counting to three, and bent her knees at the appropriate time, but every other sense was filled with him. She kept her hands on his arms after he'd already set her down on the hard surface she guessed to be his tailgate.

"Regan," his voice was gruff as he stepped closer, in between her legs.

"Hm?" She tilted her head back, no longer caring she couldn't see him.

Then his strong lips captured hers, and his arms wrapped tight around her waist. The kiss was soft, with a bit of heat that made Regan want more—and he pulled back far too soon. "Sorry," he whispered.

She shook her head, unable to keep her smile away. "Don't be."

"Want to take off your blindfold now?"

"So you're not going to kill me?" *Or kiss me again?*

"Not just yet." He kissed the tip of her nose moments before the blindfold slid loose.

Right in her line of sight was Clay, and she was okay with that. Hunky-dory, even—if she was the type of girl to say hunky-dory. Unfortunately he moved away, but in doing so she managed to see a huge billboard. No, not a billboard at all, but a giant movie screen.

She gasped and clamored to her knees to scan the area. The gravel lot was littered with cars each parked near a white post. In the distance she could see a concession stand with a small tower over it for what she assumed was the projection room.

"No way." She spun back around to set her hands on his shoulders. "A drive-in? Really?"

"Too corny?" He cracked his knuckles, shuffling his feet.

"God no, I love it!"

The tension seeped out of him, and he swiped his hand across his forehead. "Whew. I was worried I was being too big of a cheese dog."

"I like that you're cheesy. I haven't had that before." She glanced down at the admission and shook her head. "No one has worked so hard to surprise me before. So thank you."

"Never had a surprise? Really?"

Her mouth went dry. She had to change the subject immediately, or else she'd reveal too much. The past was her least favorite thing to talk about. He'd probably hate her if he knew anyway. She plastered a smile back on her face and met his gaze. "So what are we watching?"

A familiar twist of disappointment marred his bright smile for a fraction of a second. Just as quickly it disappeared and he hopped up onto the tailgate. "Mid-week they aren't as busy so they do older movies. I hope you don't mind Star Wars."

"Mind? Why on earth would I mind?"

"You never know. You might be a Star Trek snob."

"Never." She nudged him with a laugh. "I like them all. You'd better stop now while you're ahead. I'm going to think I hit the awesome jackpot, and I never ever hit the awesome jackpot, so I'll start thinking it's all a trick somehow."

"No trick. Cross my heart." He crossed his fingers over his heart. "So how about some popcorn? I brought drinks and candy. They're in the cooler back there."

A glance over her shoulder revealed a cooler strapped to the front of the truck bed so it wouldn't slide around. Strapped in beside it was a clear bag with blankets and pillows. "Well, I'm impressed. You thought of everything."

"I hope so. Once I get that popcorn I don't want to move from this spot while we watch the movie." He nudged her shoulder. "So I'll go get the popcorn, and we'll get comfy?"

"Sounds like a plan." The truck jolted when he got off. "Wait, Clay?"

He turned back. "What? You need something?"

"Just one thing." Fear made her hands shake, but she reached out anyway to tug him close.

His grin spread, and without further coaxing from her he met her kiss.

She wrapped her arms around his neck and relaxed into the warmth of his kiss. For tonight she wanted to let go of her fears, and he made it so easy by returning her kiss with enthusiasm she thought might just be genuine. When he pulled back, she actually pouted and was rewarded with his warm chuckle.

"I'll be back. Once I am and we're comfortable, I'll make sure not to stop so easy."

"I hope you don't." Heat flooded her cheeks, but she stopped herself from ducking away.

He gave her another soft kiss, and stepped back. "Be back in five."

"Okay." As he left, she exhaled a content sigh. Maybe tonight would be good after all. If she could stop second guessing every moment and relaxing just this one time, she could enjoy the evening. Then even if it all fell apart, she'd have one nice night.

Plus Star Wars.

Excitement bubbled again and she scrambled into the bed of the truck to set up the blankets.

Chapter Seven

A honking horn pulled Clay from his work. He wiped the grease from his hands as he withdrew his head out from under the car hood. After he'd waved off his mechanics, he headed toward the doors. Before he got there he spotted a bright white cowboy hat and blonde hair through the glass and grinned.

He threw open the door. "Calliope!"

"Hey big brother!" His sister spun around and wrapped him in a savage hug. "Damn, I missed you something fierce."

"Missed you too, baby sis." Clay stepped back and resumed wiping off his hands. Calliope was only ten months younger than he was, and the most fiercely independent of the bunch. Even so, a random visit near the end of May wasn't typical for her. "So are you going to tell my why you're really here? Or do I have to call Mama?"

"Mama doesn't know, so it doesn't matter if you call." Calli patted his cheek. "And my reasons are mine."

"Fat chance I'm letting you leave it at that." Clay shoved his rag into his back pocket. "Let me get cleaned up while you throw your things upstairs. We'll go have lunch."

"I'll take you up on the food, but not the conversation." Calli hauled her suitcase out of the trunk. "I'd much rather hear about the girl making you all flustered."

"You'll get better than that. You'll get to meet her. She's working today."

"Oh goody. Then be quick about it." Calli didn't give him another look as she traipsed up the side stairs to his apartment.

Clay shook his head and went inside to let the guys know he was heading for lunch. One of them decided to take off for lunch too, while his shop manager, Chris, said he'd stay behind to finish the Ellsworth's car. Clay made fast work of scrubbing his arms and face. On his way out, he dropped his hat on his head.

Calli was already waiting outside with a shit-eating grin already in place. "So she's cute, what else do you know about her?"

"Why couldn't you stay down south?" He shook his head and ignored her question, choosing instead to head to the crosswalk. "Don't you have anything better to do than harass me? Like, oh, I don't know—working or having a life of your own?"

She blew a large raspberry and turned her thumb down. "Both in the toilet, and no I don't have anything better to do. I have to keep an eye on you. After all, you haven't had a girl since that uptight girl, what was her name?"

"Casey." Clay grumbled and rubbed the back of his neck. When he'd first come to Rochester he'd met Casey at school. They'd dated for almost four years before he'd realized she'd been sleeping around behind his back from the second he'd decided to leave RIT to buy the shop. "Why on earth bring her up?"

"To point out that your head isn't always screwed on right when it comes to women."

"Well that taught me a lot, and Regan is different." He hoped.

"Well, I'll see about that."

"Myrtle loves her," Clay protested. "What else can you do?"

"Myrtle's a good gauge, but I'm your sister." Calli dragged him across the street when the light turned. He was beginning to regret suggesting they go to lunch.

"Be nice."

"I always am. That's part of my southern charm, you know. Mama didn't raise no fools."

"She raised you." He laughed when she shoved him aside. "What?"

"Jerk!" She hopped up the three steps to the diner door and let herself in.

Clay followed, still chuckling as he stepped inside The Diner. His amusement faded when he noticed for the first time just how crowded the restaurant was. So much for Calli getting to know Regan at all right then. Maybe it was for the best, it wasn't fair to corner her at work with his sister. No one deserved that.

Calli waved him to the counter where she'd managed to snag two stools for them to sit at. She grinned and scanned the restaurant. "Well?"

"Be a little more obvious, why don't you?" When she stood, he gripped her shoulder and pulled her back into her seat. "I was kidding."

"I wasn't."

"I don't see her."

Right as he spoke, Regan burst out from the kitchen with a large tray full of food. The way she held it blocked him from her view, but he recognized her instantly. Against his better judgment, he tracked her path all the way to the large corner booth.

"Oooh, she's adorably scrumptious. Are you sure she plays for your team?"

"Back off, sis." Clay was surprised at how harsh he snarled the words. "I mean, I'm sure."

"You are smitten. So tell me about her."

Clay never got the chance as Myrtle set down drinks in front of them. Myrtle circled the counter to hug Calli. "Hello there, stranger. What brings you to New York?"

"Just about everything went to hell in a hand basket, so I hightailed it up here." Calli leaned close to Myrtle. "Also wanted to check out his little filly."

Clay groaned and dropped his head into his hands.

"She's a good girl, if a bit skittish. Hard worker, and I haven't seen this boy smile so much in years." Myrtle patted Clay's hand.

He picked his head up and pursed his lips at the woman he considered like an aunt. "You're not helping. This nosy child should just leave me alone."

"She's worried about you. Nothing wrong with that." Myrtle winked. "Now I got customers. Let me get you a waitress. *Regan.*"

Calli wiggled in her seat and performed a small clap. "Oh goody."

"You said you'd behave," Clay muttered.

"That's no fun." She ran her fingers through her hair and shook it out. "Do I look okay? I like to make a good impression."

"I said back off." Clay smiled when Regan came around the counter. "If you're too swamped, we can wait."

Regan smiled and shook her head. "Not at all. You came at a good time, all of my tables have their food. I just need to keep an eye on drinks and condiments."

"Good." Clay forgot his good sense and reached across to brush his fingers with hers.

"I'm Calliope, but you can call me Calli." Calli interrupted with a spectacularly grand display of her hand between him and Regan.

"Oh." Regan startled like she'd just noticed Calli was there. While she recovered for the most part, a blush lit her cheeks as she took Calli's hand. "Clay's sister, right?"

"So he did mention me." Calli stooped so far as to flutter her eyelashes. "Well, I'll be."

"Yeah. He talks about all of you all the time." Regan blinked like she didn't know what to make of Calli, and she probably didn't. "You're the horse trainer, right?"

"That's me. It's good to meet you." Calli released her hand. "You think you can keep this guy in line?"

"Clay?" Regan furrowed her brow. "I think it's the other way around."

"Oh, darling. Don't give him so much power. Ever." Calli wagged her finger. "No man deserves that kind of power."

Regan paled and looked down at her pad. She took a deep breath and cleared her throat. "Usual, Clay?"

"Yeah." Clay furrowed his brow, concerned over how much Regan folded in on herself. "Same for Calli, but she'll take the onions I don't want."

"Got it." Regan scribbled on her pad and spun away. Before they could say anything else, she rushed off into the diner toward her other tables.

"What was that about?" Calli turned to watch Regan as she worked. "Most women joke back with me when I say that."

"I told you she was skittish, Calli." Clay folded his napkin over and over. "I don't know why yet. She doesn't talk much about herself."

"Then how do you know you like her?"

"I just do. She's funny, sarcastic, smart. Then again, she's also got a serious self-esteem problem and doesn't think she is any of those things. Every time I try to compliment her she's so shocked by it, it's weird."

"She as geeky as you?"

"Actually, yes." He winked, the smile returning. "We talk geek quite a bit. Oh, and she adopted a one eared cat because she was worried no one else would. Named her Uno."

"One-eared?"

"Yeah." Clay could still remember Regan's small admission of adopting the cat because it was broken like she was. "I took her to see Star Wars at the drive in for our first date. She absolutely loved it."

"Definitely your kind of woman, then."

"So it's your turn now that you've harassed me and embarrassed Regan somehow. Why are you here, sis? What's the disaster that befell your love life and career?"

"Ryan." Calli leaned her elbows on the counter. "Ryan happened."

"Your boss?" Clay leaned on the counter next to her. "I thought you'd sworn off sleeping around at work."

"Well, you know me."

"I do. That's why I'm surprised."

Her shoulders drooped and she let out a long breath. "That's why I came here. You'd know I meant it when I said I didn't mean for it to happen. It's not anything I meant to happen, but over the time I worked there we became good friends, close. Then we went on a road trip delivering horses in Kentucky, and it happened."

"Ryan's married."

"Yeah." She rubbed her hand over her face and sighed. "Her husband wasn't too happy. Fired me and threatened her with a divorce. She almost took him up on it, but I told her not to. I wouldn't be a home wrecker if she thought there was something still there. She did, and so I left. Figured some distance would do me good."

"I'm sorry, Calli." He squeezed her shoulder. "Really."

"Thanks. I guess it's for the best. It was stupid of me to fall for a married woman."

"Love doesn't really care about smart or stupid."

"Guess we've both learned that lesson."

"The hard way."

* * * *

Regan hadn't been surprised by the knock on her door that night, even less so to find Clay on the other side. Somehow for the rest of lunch she'd managed to avoid Clay and his sister, even to the point of someone else taking their food. A busy lunch hour had been the perfect excuse, but now she had nowhere to hide.

She forced a smile and gestured him inside. Uno trotted right up to him and curled around his legs with a forceful purr. Regan's smile grew a little stronger when he picked the cat up and snuggled it, scratching Uno under the chin, her favorite spot.

Regan quirked an eyebrow at the loud purr echoing through her hallway. "Next thing I know my little escape artist is going to be leaving the apartment to come find you."

"Nah. She knows where she belongs." He chuckled and set her down. "Sorry for just stopping by."

"It's fine. Come on in. You want anything to drink?" For some reason she was dropping into a nervous ramble. Calli's words about men having power over you were oddly reminiscent of what Grace had said to her once.

Shame over what she'd become in the past six years burned deep—even as part of her still felt she had to return to it. Life with Tony wasn't good, she knew that in her head, but she loved him, she had at least. Plus, she knew what to expect. Life was stable.

Until the day he'd hit her. Grace would tell her to remember that—always.

Still, where she was now wasn't stable. She didn't know what she was thinking half the time, much less what she was feeling. Clay was a big part of her confusion.

Clay, who was currently waving his hand in front of her face. Confusion darkened his eyes. "Regan? Did you hear me?"

"I got lost in my own head, I guess." She tried to laugh it off, but his frown grew. *Busted.*

"You do that a lot. Where do you go?"

"Nowhere. Now, did you want a drink?" She turned to go into the kitchen, but he closed his hand over her arm. The hold was gentle, but she tensed, her stomach flipping in panic.

"Let me go, please. I need a drink." She'd be more embarrassed about the tremble in her voice later.

"All right, but I'm not dropping the subject."

Of course he wouldn't, her luck didn't run that good ever. She darted into the kitchen and grabbed a soda from the fridge. She contemplated running out the back door, but what good would that do her now?

After she took a deep breath, she straightened her shoulders and headed into the living room. Clay sat on the couch, Uno perched on his shoulder, his gaze on the TV where she'd left on a rerun of *Next Generation*.

She leaned on the door frame and fiddled with the soda-tab. Instinct had her tense and ready for the scolding. She always knew when they were coming. Rather than face his hotness and let it fluster her further, she kept her eyes on the worn carpet.

"What are you doing over there?"

"Waiting."

"For what?"

Silence was her best answer, so that's what she gave. When the silence dragged on, her nerves bundled into a living force that scratched its way up her esophagus until she squeaked. "I'm sorry."

"What are you apologizing for?"

"I don't know." The pressure of her tears threatened to burst forth and she screwed her eyes shut. Tears didn't work, not ever. If anything, they made the situation worse. She shoved them back down until she was sure she could open her eyes without crying. The familiar calm of numbing her emotions took over and she took a deep breath.

"Regan, come here."

Still unwilling to meet his gaze, she only lifted her head a few inches to find him patting the couch next to him. On automation, she did as instructed, and perched on the edge of the couch.

His warm hand settled on hers, and when she jumped, he scooted closer. "What's going on? I just came over to talk, and apologize for my sister's behavior. She doesn't exactly have the best manners in our family."

"She didn't do anything." Once again her voice strained to be heard. She took a large swig of her soda to try to regain her ability to speak.

"She comes off as overbearing, I know."

Regan worried her lip between her teeth and set the can on the coffee table. If only he'd just say it, she hated having it dragged out like this.

"I'm sorry for her anyway."

"Really, she was fine. Nothing I haven't heard before. I was just really busy."

This time his silence lingered, as well as his hand on hers. She didn't know why she hadn't pulled away yet, except that she hoped it meant this wouldn't go downhill. Maybe it should, though. Clay was way out of her league; she'd known that all along.

He touched his finger to her chin and drew her gaze to his. "Right there. Where do you go? There is so much pain in your eyes when you go away."

Every bit of air sucked out of her chest and she couldn't speak. Hot spikes of tears jabbed at her eyes, threatening to break through her years of carefully built preventatives against them. She shook her head and jerked back from his touch. "Excuse me?"

"I don't like seeing you in pain. I also—"

"Also what?" Her hands shook and she backed up further until she hit the arm of the couch. She ripped her gaze from his and tried to figure out what he was getting at, and how to accommodate him while figuring out another escape.

"I want to know you more. I know the good parts of you, but you hide so much from me. From everyone, really."

"There's nothing more to tell than what you already know."

"That's doubtful."

She rose, wringing her hands together. Uno mewled and leaped from Clay's lap and came to weave between Regan's legs. Regan took a deep breath. "You know what's important. I was born in California, went to high school in Illinois. My family and I don't get along, and now I'm here. That's me."

"You're more than that. I've seen plenty more, but I want to know more. I want to know you. I like you. A lot."

Every breath came so rapid she couldn't catch it. She shook her head.

"I thought you were getting used to that by now. We've been on four dates already. I've told you all about me."

"Good for you!" The shout erupted without warning, and she clapped her hands over her mouth in shock. Trembling, she turned toward him with wide eyes. His hands were raised and he appeared to be as surprised as she was at her fit of temper.

"I thought it was mutual."

"It was. Is. I." Bile rose and she turned away. "I don't like to talk about the past. It's the past, don't you get that? You know everything about me that matters. Everything that's important, anyway."

"Why didn't you ever tell me you danced?"

Every inch of her went cold, pain lanced her heart. She'd given up on dance so long ago, at least that anyone had seen. She still watched *Dance For Your Life* and any other modern dance show she could to keep up on trends, but it was a foolish dream. Her parents had reminded her of that often enough that she knew it. Dancing was her thing, hers alone. "That's private."

"What?"

"It's mine. I'm not good, I just do it for fun. How did you know?"

"I was working late one night when you were closing at The Diner. On my way outside to head upstairs I saw you." His feet appeared in her line of sight. "I have to tell you something."

"No. You don't." Regan took a deep breath.

"I don't date a lot of people. I got my heart broke once. I told you about Casey."

"Please stop."

"When we went to lunch at The Midway that day and talked all through lunch, I started liking you. I thought you maybe did too."

She clenched her jaw tight, but had a compulsion to nod her agreement.

"When I asked you out, I meant it for real. I like you. Your humor, your sarcasm, that you're smarter than you give yourself credit for. I also thought maybe you'd let me in. If we are going to go any further, you have to let me in."

"I can't. There's nothing there. I'm not whatever you've made me up to be in your mind. This is me and I don't want to talk about my past. It's nothing you want to know."

"Yes it is."

Her fist clenched so tight her nails dug into her palm. "You asked me to trust you enough on our first date to blindfold me and drive me to a strange place. Now trust me."

"I do, but Regan—"

"Not everyone has a picture perfect childhood! Don't you get that? Not everyone on this planet can look back at the recent past and glow with accounts of family, friends and places that just leave them dreamy in happiness. We aren't all that lucky, Clay."

His jaw went slack. "I didn't say they did."

"So not everyone wants to share campfire stories about their stupidity or triumphs and how their family and friends rallied around them. Neither do I." She turned away as the first tear fell.

"Regan."

"Go away." When he touched her shoulder, she jerked away. She darted around him and down the hall to her bathroom. Once inside she slammed the door shut and locked it.

Clay knocked on the door. "Regan."

"Go away!"

Silence greeted her, but his shadow lingered in the hall.

"Just go. Please, go away."

"Please talk to me."

"No!" She slapped the door hard. "Go now. Leave me alone!"

"Regan."

"I can't give you what you want. Just go." She leaned back against the shower door and sank to the floor as the tears flowed. Part of her wished he'd used his mechanical smarts to unlock the door and comfort her.

Instead, he did as she asked. After about ten minutes, his shadow disappeared from the door.

She let out a deep sob and released the pent-up tears.

Chapter Eight

Regan sat on the brick wall outside the small natural food store and café and sipped her iced latte. In the three days since their fight, she and Clay had managed to mostly avoid each other.

Truth be told, she hated it. She'd missed him more than she cared to admit. She'd not known him terribly long, but it felt so good to have someone she might consider even just a friend—if not more. And not having him around wasn't much fun either.

When she'd emerged from the bathroom almost two hours after locking herself inside she'd found Uno curled up on the brim of his cowboy hat. He'd set a note on top, one she could remember word for word after reading it so many times.

Regan,

I'm sorry. I never should have pushed so hard. We've only known each other a month, and it was unfair of me to do that to you. I won't waste time or ink explaining my reasons, because they don't matter.

Just know I'm sorry.

I'm leaving my hat, the cliché of me in one accessory. I'll let you have the time you need, but if you think you can forgive me, return the hat. If not, keep it.

I care for you. If nothing else, I hope I can be your friend.

~Clay

She'd felt even worse after reading the note. He wasn't the one to blame, she didn't need to be scolded to know that.

Somehow she had to make herself talk to him. He deserved that much.

Problem was she was horrible at confrontation—as if the other night wasn't proof enough of that. The real surprise of the night was that she had spoken up in her own defense. Never once had she done that before, and she didn't know why she had with Clay.

Her attempts to reach Grace had failed, and Regan couldn't be more confused on what to do. Myrtle would tell her to listen to her heart, but that hadn't ever served her well before. Her gaze wandered to Clay's shop, and she sighed.

A voice with a familiar southern lilt startled Regan. "My brother is a big dope sometimes." Calli hopped down the steps behind her before hiking herself up on the brick wall beside Regan.

Regan took a long sip of her drink, unsure what to say.

"He's all heart and no brains most of the time. Then again, I guess that's better than a man that thinks with his dick first." Calli swung her legs back and forth. "You okay?"

"Yeah." It wasn't fully heart-felt and Regan knew it. She shrugged. "I guess."

"Sorry about what I said the other day." Calli stared at her own feet as she lifted them. When they dropped she glanced at Regan. "There are a lot of bad guys out there. I'm guessing you know that."

Regan pursed her lips and turned away.

"Clay isn't one of them, but I guess you know that too." Calli's hand settled on Regan's shoulder. "Avoiding the good doesn't make the bad go away."

Tension raced through Regan, but before she could respond, Calli had jumped off the wall. Regan took a shaky breath. "It's not his fault, you know."

"It's not yours either, sugar." Calli waved over her shoulder, not looking back. A few minutes later she'd turned the corner onto the square.

Alone again, Regan returned her gaze to Clay's shop. Even a block away, she could hear the power tools running inside the open doors of the shop. There was every chance that he wouldn't want to see her again after the way she'd treated him.

She looked where Calli had disappeared again, then took a deep breath and hopped off the brick wall. If nothing else, she had to apologize. Nerves clawed in her belly so fierce, she had to toss away her drink.

There was no traffic on the street, so she ignored the cross walk and rushed across. She kept her pace fast so she wouldn't lose what little courage she had. Even so, her hands were shaking by the time she got to the shop.

Unable to force herself inside, she lingered outside the building in the alley between it and the neighboring strip mall. She rubbed her hands on her shorts to try to steady them. *Chicken shit. You've always been such a chicken shit. You swore you'd change.*

She had sworn, but it turned out change was so much harder than a simple vow. Social situations with strangers, and confrontations, had done her in since childhood. It drove her father crazy when she'd dissolved into tears every time he confronted her, even about little things like if she'd done her homework.

In the years since she'd manage to gain some control on her tears, but not on the internal vice-like grip of panic. The tightening of her vocal chords that so often frustrated her into tears, and the tears themselves, always made her feel worse until she walked away from the situation all together.

This time had to be different.

She clenched her hands into fists to still them and took a deep breath. An apology was necessary, and what was more important—she didn't want Clay out of her life. Maybe there could have been something there, something more than she'd had before.

With a deep breath, she turned and strode into the garage so fast, the sudden difference in lighting momentarily blinded her. By the time her eyes adjusted, all the tools had stopped running and silence reigned inside the garage.

Heat rose to her cheeks as the mechanics stared at her. After a minute two of them shrugged and went back to work, but one walked forward. "May I help you?"

"Regan." Clay stood just outside his office door, his expression hidden under a new cowboy hat, though he'd sounded surprised.

Regan smiled at the mechanic who'd taken that as his clue to go back to work. Before she could form a sentence, the familiar strangulation of her vocal chords returned. To make matters worse, Clay was heading her direction and she was wondering if she'd been insane to do this.

He stopped a few feet away, his boots in her line of vision. "I—Hi."

The idea he might be nervous too boosted her hope just enough for her to lift her head. His gaze was on her hands, the remnants of a smile fading every second. She looked down at her hands and gasped. The hat wasn't with her. "Your hat. I—I didn't expect to come here."

"Oh." The screech of a tool made them both jump, and he frowned. "Why don't we go to my office? It's quieter there."

And less public. She nodded fiercely. "Yes, please. I'm sorry."

His brow furrowed, but he didn't respond. Instead, his hand settled under her elbow and he led her to his office. Once inside, he closed the door on another mechanical screech, muting the world almost into silence. "I'm happy to see you."

She smiled at her own hands as they twisted in front of her. Warmth filled her belly and eased some of her nerves.

Some, but not all. She cleared her throat to try to restore her ability to speak like a human. "I'm sorry."

"No. You don't have to be."

"Yes, I do."

"No. I'm sorry."

"You weren't entirely wrong." The last word escaped in a half-shriek and she was grateful his office was sound protected.

He sat on the edge of his desk. His hat had been removed and so he'd focused his gaze on her. "I shouldn't have pushed."

"Maybe, but you weren't wrong." Regan took a deep breath to brace herself and crossed to the couch. She sat, staring at the window into the shop. "I like you too. I just—I haven't had much experience with dating."

"How is that possible?" He crossed to sit near her, but stayed on the opposite side of the couch. "I don't get that."

"It's true." She squeezed her knees, then forced herself to turn to face him. A twist in her stomach formed, but she pushed past it. "I—I want to try to tell you more, but you have to give me time. I don't like thinking about most of what I was."

"You don't have to."

"Yes. I do. Please, please, please don't argue with me." Arguing or protesting would make the whole thing harder. She clenched her fists on her lap. "You're right, we've only known each other a month, but we were dating. I'm just not good at it."

He scooted closer and set his hand on top of her clenched one. "Hey. I thought you were doing pretty good."

She smiled and shook her head. "Not good enough."

"I didn't mean to make you feel that way."

"It's okay." She unclenched her hands and took a deep breath.

"What now?"

"I don't know." All the nervous energy that had begun to fade rose up again. "Before you make a suggestion, you should know something about me."

"What?"

She opened her mouth to tell him everything, but the words wouldn't form. There was no way in hell she was ready for that confession. She flew to her feet and wrung her hands, scrambling for words to satisfy the conversation. "My family."

To his credit, he didn't follow her, or try to push out her words. He remained on the couch, his forearms on his knees. When she glanced his way, he only smiled encouragement.

"My dancing." She changed the subject again. After a deep breath, she exhaled the tension away. "It's something I do just for me, for fun. I'm not any good."

"May I?" He lifted a finger, asking permission to interject. At her nod, he rose. "I don't know much about dancing, but Cadence makes me watch that *Dance For Your Life* show whenever she comes for a visit. What I saw when you danced, looked every bit as good as the folks I see on that show."

The compliment simultaneously pleased and embarrassed her, and she ducked her head to try to cope with the confusing conflict of emotions. "You're sweet, but maybe biased."

"Maybe, but I stand by what I said."

"Well, either way, I only started dancing because my parents were tired of me whining that my brother had sports, which I absolutely hated and suck at, by the way." She tucked a loose lock of hair behind her ear. "So they put me in dance. Pretty sure they didn't expect me to like it, either, or they might not have."

When she met his gaze, there wasn't doubt or judgment anywhere to be found. His brow puckered in concern, or maybe confusion, but there was none of the exasperation or disbelief she was used to when she made such statements. "Why do you say that?"

"Dancing isn't a career choice. You have to be the best to even consider it. You really need something to fall back on. A *real* job, a *real* career, a *real* degree." The whole statement spilled from her lips with the bitterness of the bile that rose in her throat. "Hearing that regularly told me how good they thought I was. I learned to dance on my own time, and went to school for what they wanted. Flunked out, though. Guess I wasn't so smart after all."

"Maybe you were. You knew you weren't doing what you wanted." A smile started to curve his lips and her fears went away in that moment. "I knew I wasn't. Granted, I didn't rebel as strong as you did, but I did leave school to buy this place."

"I still haven't figured out what I want."

"And I bet your parents haven't figured out why you did the same as me. Why you gave it up to follow your heart."

"But I didn't. I'm not dancing."

"Sure you are. You just dance when no one is watching."

She pursed her lips. "Or when I think no one is watching."

He had the decency to look embarrassed, although his smile didn't waiver. "It was an accident. And I didn't stay long, though I wanted to keep watching. I could tell you didn't want to be seen. I don't like intruding where I'm not wanted."

"That's why you left."

"You told me to go away. I didn't want to, but I had pushed enough."

"Everyone always pushes."

* * * *

Clay didn't quite know how to take that. There was so much feeling behind the whispered statement, he was curious as to what had happened to her. Still, he'd learned his lesson. He set his hands on her shoulders and waited for her to look up again. "I won't. Or rather, I'll try not to. I want to know more about you, but I'll follow your pace."

Her shoulders sagged and she shook her head. "You shouldn't have to beg to know me. That isn't fair."

"Sure it is." He pulled her closer, and the suddenness of the action made her gasp. "The point of dating is getting to know each other. Some people are disgustingly open about themselves, others aren't. That's life."

A slow smile started to cross her features, and for the first time in days, it reached her eyes. She lifted a brow. "Says one disgustingly open man."

"I know. I'm horrifying. I understand if you want nothing more to do with me and my disturbing tendency toward telling you every detail of my life."

Panic replaced her smile and her fingers dug into his back. "I don't want that."

"Then you should have brought my hat." His stab at a humorous reply had the intended effect, and she began to relax again. "After all, you had me worried."

"What if I want to keep it anyway?" She smiled even as red seeped into her cheeks. "And maybe still see if we can make this dating thing work?"

"Guess I don't mind." He felt a ripple of pleasure that she wanted to keep his hat. "As far as this dating thing? I definitely want to make it work."

"I don't like fighting. I'm not good at confrontation."

"You did pretty well the other night. You held your own."

"I don't know how. I never have before."

Ten thousand questions leaped into his head, but he bit his tongue to hold them back. After dissecting the comment for a few minutes, he found the silver lining. "Then maybe that's a good sign. You're comfortable enough with me to yell at me."

"But I've only known you a month."

"Then I like my odds going forward." He winked, laughing when she managed to smile again. "Can we start now? How about lunch?"

She opened her mouth and he sensed a protest coming, but then her stomach growled so loud they both looked at it. Her laughter was such a welcome break to the tension, he joined her. She grabbed her stomach and shrugged. "I guess I don't have a say in the matter today."

"You were going to turn me down?"

"I was only concerned about you getting your work done."

"I've been working late the past couple of nights," he admitted. "I couldn't sleep well, so I got us all caught up, minus the two cars out there. One of them just came in today, the other is a two week job on a good day."

"Only if you're sure." She set her hands on her hips. "I might have the day off, but you don't. We could always meet after work."

He thrilled at the way she blushed at her own bold suggestion. "We can do both."

"I thought you weren't going to push your luck anymore."

"Somehow I don't think I am." He grinned and pulled open the door to the shop. Anything she might have tried to retort with got lost in the chaos of running tools. After he'd caught Chris' eye and mimed eating, he led Regan from the shop to his truck.

"Where are we going that requires a vehicle?"

"I thought we'd pick up a box picnic at the grocery store and go eat lakeside. In the shade of the trees in Lakeside Park the heat isn't so bad." He got in the truck and waited for her to join him before he started it up. "Unless you have a better idea."

"Actually, no. Sounds better than the fast food I was going to suggest." She settled in and turned her attention out the window. This time when she disappeared, her hand settled on his.

He laced his fingers with hers and gave them a squeeze. The whole way to the grocery store they held hands. Inside they nitpicked over the lunch choices available until they'd managed to get the deli counter to make a special box with foods containing no onions.

When they got back in the truck, she was laughing.

"What?"

"I just never met anyone that hates onions as much as I do. That allergy line really does shut them up every time. I just can't get over that. My life would have been easier years ago if I'd thought to use it."

"In this day and age everyone is afraid of being sued over stuff like that. You say allergy and they drop everything. Wouldn't have worked as well when we were kids, but it sure does now." He draped his arm across the back of the seat, driving out of the parking lot toward Lakeside Park. He was glad things had smoothed over for now. Somehow he didn't think they were done struggling over her past, but he'd be satisfied with baby steps.

She remained quiet until they got to the park and had been set up at a picnic table closest to the water while still shaded. As they dove into the cold fried chicken, she met his gaze. "How many girlfriends have you had?"

Surprised by the intentional question about his past, he set down his chicken and wiped his hands while he thought. He didn't want to lie, so he had to think about it. "Do you mean serious girlfriends, or people I've dated?"

"Um. I guess both." She plucked at the crispy skin, and popped a piece into her mouth. "Anyone you dated longer than we've been dating."

"We've only been dating a couple of weeks."

"Okay, longer than a month, then." She chewed on her lip, staring down the chicken leg in her hand.

"All right. Let's see, I started dating at sixteen." He took a long drink of his pop, surprised when he realized his answer. "Well, it's not a lot. For two years in high school I dated four girls, only one was serious. We dated for a year, broke up after graduation."

She blinked a few times in silence. When she spoke, her voice expressed a few thousand acres worth of doubt. "Really?"

"Yeah. Then in college I dated three, maybe. The third being Casey." He smiled. "And now there's you. I don't think there's anyone I can think of that I only dated once or twice. I don't date willy-nilly."

"Oh." Fast as she ducked her head, she couldn't hide her smile.

"Can I ask the same question of you?"

"I, um." Her eyes darted back and forth, and he thought she might say no, but then she nodded. "I think so."

"You think so? Do you not know how many?"

"No, I know. I just—I guess it's not if you can ask, but if I can answer." Already she was retreating, not enough to make him force a subject change, but enough to see talking about guys was as tough as talking about her family.

"If you can't, I can try to guess."

Her eyes lit up and she nodded. "That might help."

"Okay, let's see." He rubbed his hands together, and grinned. "I'm not a carney by trade, so I have to warm up my talents."

She giggled when he set his fingers to his temples. "Really?"

"Shh. You're interrupting my communication with the spirits." He cracked an eye open enough to see she was enjoying the show. With a chuckle, he closed it again. She'd said she didn't have experience, and had been surprised at his number. It must be close. "You've dated three guys."

Her silence spoke well enough for his accuracy, and when he opened his eyes, she was pale, but nodding. "Yes."

"I'm going to say, two were serious?"

"No. Just the one." Her voice cracked and she started to dig through the basket.

Rather than push further, Clay changed the subject, although his mind stayed puzzling over her words. *Just the one.*

Chapter Nine

Clay whistled as he pulled on his boots. After another month of dating Regan, they'd made some progress, but it was as slow as he'd expected. What he hadn't expected was his continuing frustration at the giant road block she kept up.

It was almost as if she had over half of herself guarded behind a steel wall. He was patient, waiting didn't bother him. What bothered him was how much pain was associated with it, and the strong sense that it was something he should know. The way she kept trying to say something to him, and stopping herself didn't help.

"Lordy, I forgot how annoying you are when you're in love. That incessant whistling will be the death of me." Calli stepped out of the bathroom, brush in hand. She pointed it at him. "Why did I help you again?"

"Because you love me." He grinned at her, then did a double take. "Wait, what? Who said anything about love?"

"Please. This is me you're talking to." Calli sat next to him and nudged his shoulder. "Unlike me, you don't date around, you rarely date in general, and even then it's only with someone you feel connected to. Getting to know the girl only made you fall head over heels. You're just waiting for her to catch up before you dare to admit it."

If she'd been even a little wrong, he might have protested. As it stood, she was spot on. Despite all of his reservations about what she was hiding from him, everything he did know about her, he loved. Shockingly, they'd had a lot more in common than he'd ever expected.

"Clay."

He looked up in surprise at her serious tone. "What?"

She opened her mouth, but then closed it. After a minute she took a deep breath. "I'm happy for you. Just remember to think with your brain as well as your heart."

"You saying you don't like her?" If that was the case, Clay would be shocked. In the past month, Calli had become as friendly with Regan as Roni. If he didn't know his sister better, he'd be worried she was trying to swing Regan to her side.

"No. I'm saying love is blind and you might miss some things, like you did before."

Unease trembled through him, but before he could ask Calli what she meant, there was a knock at the door. He rose after a kiss to Calli's cheek. "I'll be careful."

"And I won't wait up. I stuck a few extras in your wallet, just in case."

"You're a pig, Calli. A real pig."

"Always." She laughed and disappeared back into the bathroom.

Still chuckling, Clay pulled open the door to find Regan with her back to the door, looking out from the railing. "What are you staring at?"

"Nothing in particular. I just like the view from here. You can see the town square and the lights from the boats on the lake. Too bad it's not bigger, you could just sit out here and relax sometimes." Regan smiled when he joined her. "Are you ready?"

"I sure am. Where are we heading to?" Tonight's date was all her idea, and she'd even borrowed a car for it. He had to admit, his curiosity was piqued.

"Nope. Sorry. It's my turn to surprise you." Her smile faltered. "I just hope you like it."

"I have no doubt that I'm going to love it." He laced his fingers with hers. "But I could have driven if you wanted."

"No. It's a borrowed car, but I'm still glad to be driving even for just a night. Besides, then I'd have to tell you where we were going, and you might guess what we were doing."

"I know."

She chuckled, slipping into the car when he held the door open for her. By the time he got around and in his seat, she was still laughing. "I know I'm bad with surprises, but it seems that you aren't much better."

"I'm really not. I'll probably try to guess the whole way there."

"You'll try, but I doubt you will."

Turned out they were both right, as he laid guesses on her for the full thirty minute drive to the next suburb over, through dinner, and back into the car. To his chagrin, and her enjoyment, he failed miserably. She surprised him by not heading back toward town, but into Rochester. By then, she was biting her lip, no longer jokingly answering his guesses.

He ventured another guess. "Are you lost?"

"No, not yet anyway. I just don't want to miss the—there it is." She turned off onto a side street, and then another. Rather than risk getting lost, he let her drive in peace and quiet until she pulled into a parking lot and breathed a sigh of relief. "I was afraid I'd forget where I was going, and I haven't gotten a smart phone yet."

"The movies?" Clay leaned down to get a better view of the theater.

"Just come on. Oh, and you should probably leave your hat in here, just to be safe."

"Safe?" He couldn't even begin to imagine what she meant by that.

"You heard me." She reached over the seat to grab a bag from the back, and then got out of the car. "It took me a week to find out where this was going on. I almost gave up hope, really."

"Hope for what?" The moment they turned the corner, he realized what she meant. No wonder she'd gone to the parking lot the back way. The brightly costumed people in front of the theater gave away the game. Men in drag, women in gold sequined hats and jackets with striped shorts, boas and motorcycle jackets abounded. "Rocky Horror!"

She grinned. "You bet. Is that okay?"

"Yes, definitely. Thanks for telling me to leave my hat behind." He pulled her close. "I haven't been to a showing of this since high school."

"Me either, actually. I brought supplies, though." She tapped the bag. "Toast, TP, newspapers, and rice."

"You're prepared."

"I hope so." She winked as the line started to move. "Let's go."

Clay didn't argue, following her in and helping her find a decent seat halfway up the rows. When she insisted on sitting on the end, he didn't argue. They got settled in and once the movie started, they both joined in the calls at the screen.

Even as rice poured down his back and into his jeans, Clay couldn't have been happier. The night was proving fun and crazy as any Rocky Horror show did. The best part came during the Time Warp, though.

Out of nowhere beside him, the shy, inhibited woman he'd come to know burst up from her seat to join the group on stage in front of the screen. As they reenacted the scene, she danced step for step alongside Columbia, with a pair of sequined taps to match.

Clay whistled and cheered for Regan. He was too impressed for his shock to last long. When Regan returned to their seats, her face flushed, he couldn't contain himself. He dragged her close and kissed her deeply.

She sagged against him, her fingers burrowing in his hair. Her tongue danced with his eagerly before she pulled back slowly. "Well hello to you too, cowboy."

"That was impressive."

"Lots of people do it."

"Just shut up and take the compliment."

She smiled and nodded. "Okay."

He winked and gave her another quick kiss before he leaned in close as the shouts around them grew louder again. "Let's finish this, and then I want to kiss you more."

"Kiss me and more?"

When she pulled back enough to meet his gaze, he brushed his thumb along her cheekbone. He smiled. "Only if you want."

"I do."

The whole theater yelled, "Are you a hooker?"

Regan busted into laughter and squeezed his hand. After another wink, she turned back to the screen, but her hand remained secure in his.

* * * *

Regan held her finger to her lips as they got closer to her apartment. She'd dropped the car off at Myrtle's a few blocks over, so as to not wake Mrs. Bell with their arrival. The logical side of her brain told her to send Clay home, but something else told her to let him come over even though it was the middle of the night.

Truth be told, she didn't know if it was her heart or her libido telling her to let him come by, and giddy off of the fun of their evening, she no longer cared. She was exhausted from overthinking every move she made. After years of stepping carefully, just for once she wanted to let loose again.

Sure it was bound to wind her in another mess of trouble, but Clay didn't seem the kind. At least she hoped he wasn't. With Tony she'd been too young and stupid to see the signs until they'd been pointed out to her years later by Grace. This time she was wiser.

Still, her hand shook when she unlocked the door and she almost shooed him off. Instead, she took a deep breath and let him in. "Can I get you a drink? No alcohol, I'm not used to company that drinks, but I've got soda and water."

"I'm good." If he was anywhere near as wound up as she was, he gave no sign that she could see.

As if you're good at reading signals. She winced at her inner voice, and took a deep breath. "You sure? I'm grabbing one."

"I'm sure."

Regan darted into the kitchen and threw open the fridge. She soaked the cold in eagerly before grabbing a can from the top shelf. Just inviting Clay back to the apartment had her flustered, did she really think she could go through with anything?

The whole of her experience with men came down to Tony, and that wasn't anything to crow about. The mere thought of sex had her blushing so hard she could feel her skin blotching down to her chest. She probably looked like a freak.

She took several deep breaths to try to calm herself. Them coming back here didn't have to lead anywhere, after all, he might not want to. But then again, if he didn't, her embarrassment would be rooted in a whole other issue. One she was far too familiar with and knew she could handle.

After she'd cracked open the soda, she took a long swig before she dared venture into the living room. Clay was sitting on the couch, grinning as he flipped the sequined top hat she'd kept in her bag around in his fingers.

She sat near him on the couch, his grin too contagious for her to hold onto her nerves. "What?"

"I'm just remembering you up on that stage. That was pretty awesome." He turned his head to meet her gaze. "What made you think Rocky Horror?"

"I don't know. I used to go with friends in high school. I just hoped we had that much in common that you'd like it too." She dragged her gaze away, chewing her lip as she played with the soda tab. "And I guess it was a viable excuse to dance."

"I didn't know you tapped, too. You put the girl playing Columbia through her paces. How'd you manage to get up there?"

She shrugged, her grin forming again. "I've been planning it for a few weeks now. Ever since our fight, I guess. First I had to find the group, then let them convince me to come up for a number. It's been a while since I'd done it. I was worried I'd forget."

"I'd say you did fine." He set his hand on her forearm. "Thank you."

Her stomach did a nervous little jump, but she managed to lift her gaze to his. "Not sure what you're thanking me for."

"For sharing that. I know you said your dancing is private—something just for you."

All the air left her lungs as she fought against the urge to hide her confession. She set down the can of soda and set her hand on his. "I wanted to share it. With you, I mean."

The smile that lit his face warmed her to the soul, and her nerves flew away. He brushed his fingers along her cheek. "That means a lot."

She nodded fiercely, too choked up to speak for a minute.

"So thank you."

"No." She exhaled slowly and clasped his other hand in hers. If there would ever be a time to tell him about her past, it would be now. Yet when she opened her mouth, she couldn't form the words again. Shame rushed forward and made her thoroughly tense again.

"Hey." He extricated a hand so he could wrap his arm around her shoulders. "Easy. I'm not asking questions right now. Just relax."

"You shouldn't have to ask." She sighed and snuggled into the crook of his shoulder. "I thought if I could show you that, I could tell you anything."

He shrugged against the back of her head. "You will. I'm not going anywhere."

"It's not about you, you know." She tilted her head to look up at him. The curl of his lip made her giggle. "That sounded horribly cliché, didn't it?"

"It sounded like the start of the 'it's not you, it's me' talk."

"It's not the talk, but it is like that. You make me feel…"

"Feel what?"

"Lots of things." She pulled her gaze away, unable to take his intensity under the weight of her own shyness. "But I know you wouldn't judge me, at least I hope you wouldn't. I just—I guess I'm not able to be okay with myself yet."

"Why don't you let me be okay with you, then?" He hooked his finger under her chin and winked. "I'm already there, maybe further than that."

"Further than okay?"

"Oh yeah." He tugged her into a gentle kiss, warm and soft. Each caress of his tongue against hers drew her deeper until her body came alive and turned to jelly all at once. When he pulled out of the kiss, he took a ragged breath. "Maybe I shouldn't have done that."

"Maybe you should have." She tipped off his hat and tossed it across the room. As she scooted closer, she scratched her nails along his scalp. "I liked it a lot."

"Regan." His eyes closed as he set his forehead against hers. Another shaky breath escaped before he spoke. "I liked it too much. I won't push you, but it'll be hard not to if we keep going."

The dose of reality tweaked her nerves enough to make her pull back an inch. She'd let him close and he hadn't laughed at her. She didn't want to stop. She was an adult, damn it, and allowed to have sex. "There are two things before I decide, or you decide, what to do next."

"Two?" He didn't let go of her wrists when she pulled back, keeping her hands close against her chest. "Okay. What's the first thing?"

"You should know." She stared at her hands where they rested on his chest. Maybe he didn't have to know, but she wanted him to know. If she liked him enough to sleep with him, she should be okay telling him she had little experience in bed. "I've only ever been with one guy."

"Does that mean I have a lot to live up to? Or just a wee, tiny bit?"

She snorted, her grin forming as she lifted her head again. "Sure you want to know?"

"Uh, not really." He chuckled and tugged her close again. When her body was flush against his, he kissed her gently. "I actually like that. If it helps, I've only been with two."

"It does a little."

"What's number two?"

She bit her lip. "I hadn't planned on bringing you back here. I don't have anything...so, do you have protection?"

His lips pursed and twisted until he chuckled. "So long as you promise to not tell my sister I'm glad she's the pervert she is and put them in my wallet."

Regan sat straight and cocked a brow at him. "Your sister supplied you with protection?"

"I was trying not to be presumptuous." Clay grinned. "Just like you."

"I'd die if my brother was that open with me." She giggled and leaned against him again. "But in this case, I guess, I'm glad your sister has no such reservations."

"But that did sort of ruin the mood, didn't it?"

"For the moment."

"Anything to be done to bring it back?"

"Hmmm." She thought for a moment. A bold idea so unlike herself she was shocked by its arrival popped into her head. Did she dare do something so blatant? "I might have an idea. It might be total idiocy, but it might just work."

"Now I'm curious." He brushed his lips in a gentle kiss. "What do we do?"

"You don't have to do anything." She slipped from his arms and crossed to the room. On the way she lit candles, and flipped off the light.

Candlelight flickered across the radio when she turned it on. After several tries she found a station that she knew played good music. Tension raced through her body, but she tried to keep it at bay, reminding herself he'd already seen her dance twice now, and this was no different.

Forget he's there, just dance. She closed her eyes to help obey her own command. For weeks she'd danced alone in this room, so she knew the layout well enough. For several moments she remained still and let the music filter in.

Once she had the beat, she began to sway her hips. Little by little she let the music take over and the familiar beat carry her through moves she'd done hundreds of times. Within three sets of eight count she'd forgotten almost everything but the music.

Unlike when she was alone, though, she couldn't ignore the strong stare of Clay. By then he was leaning forward, arms on his knees. Nothing she did escaped his gaze, and instead of making her more nervous, it thrilled her.

Every time she bent, swayed, turned or dropped, she found his unwavering stare. By the time the second song came on, she was standing in front of him. When he set his hands on her swaying hips, her heart skipped a beat. She smiled. "Mood returned?"

"Hell yes."

She bent her knees just enough to swing her hips left. It set her heart pounding when his gaze followed. "You sure?"

He tugged her closer and lifted her shirt enough to kiss her stomach. Shocking heat tore through her right to her core, and she whimpered. He nipped the flesh and pulled her to straddle his lap.

Without any guidance, she sank down and crushed her lips to his. There was no room for nerves any longer, only wandering hands and lips. Clay took his time, and she was glad to let him, all her fears falling away under his gentle guidance.

Chapter Ten

Regan tried to ignore the light streaming through the thin curtains covering her high windows. She didn't have to work until one, and Clay was still lying beside her with his arm around her waist. Clay hadn't had much to compete with, but now she wasn't sure any man could ever compare.

Not just the sex—which, wow, she had no idea it could be like that. No, he just made her feel safe, like he'd never judge her for anything. If anything, he'd look at her with too kind an eye every time.

She still had no idea what to make of that. It made her feel loved.

Like she hadn't known what love was her whole life, and maybe she hadn't. Not in years, anyway. How had she let herself miss this before? How could she have believed that what she'd had was love?

Clay's thumb brushed along her stomach, and she found him watching her. "Where'd you go just then?"

She sighed and turned toward him. Now she should tell him, tell him everything. "I made a mistake once, and I got lost in it. I'm ashamed by what I've done, and how I ended up here."

His brow puckered, and he propped himself on his elbow. "Ashamed by this?"

"No! God, no." When he relaxed, she set her hand on his. "Not by you. No, by—"

Gravel crunched outside the window, pulling Regan's attention away. She frowned, the gravel driveway was for the apartment. The only visitor she ever had was Clay. A car door closed and someone crunched along toward her door.

"Shit." Regan leaped from the bed and threw on her robe. When the expected knock came on the door, she found Clay already halfway decent in his pants.

He gathered up Uno. "I'll make sure she doesn't escape. We aren't done, you know."

"No, we aren't. I'm ready to tell you." She smiled and backed for the door, admiring his body the whole way there. With regret she backed through the door and closed it, sighing through the next knock. "I'm coming."

The voice that echoed through the door was one she'd have been happy never hearing again, and stopped her heart cold. Tony yelled, "You'd better be!"

Her heart leaped into her throat and she stood stock still in place. Every inch of her body trembled, the security of last night shaking onto the floor along with every bit of her strength. "No, please no."

"Amanda. Mandy? Open the damn door." Tony pounded again, and she heard some racket in her living room.

God, what did Clay think of this? She'd just been about to tell him everything. Instead, she inched toward the door, she knew she had to let him in. What she'd done was wrong, after all, she'd loved him, she did love him. No, she didn't. Did she?

Just as she reached for the doorknob, she heard the door to her living room open. At the same time, Tony spoke again. "Remember me? The fiancé you abandoned?"

She closed her eyes against the tears and turned the deadbolt. "I'm right here. You don't have to yell, Tony."

"How could you do this, Mandy?" He pounded on the door so it rattled too hard for her to open immediately.

She glanced over her shoulder, but only saw the back door closing on her. Everything inside her crumbled, and she opened the door. "I'm sorry."

Tony's patronizing smile greeted her, as did the ring she'd thrown down the sink. "You lost something, Mandy. Or wait, that weird lady said you went by Regan here. You really work at that greasy spoon?"

"You talked to Myrtle?" Every word squeaked, and she eyed the ring as he held it to her. No matter how much she knew she should, she couldn't lift her hands to take it back.

"Had to find out where you lived. Finding where you worked was easy, you know. Same social security number, it just took a few weeks for you to show up." He pushed his way into the apartment. When Uno mewed at him, he shoved her aside with his foot. "Ugh. A cat? And what the hell is up with her ears?"

"She was abused, don't kick her." Regan rushed forward to grab Uno away from him. She backed up against the wall. "I need you to leave, Tony."

"No, baby. I'm not going anywhere without you. We've got our lives back in Illinois. You can't tell me you like it here."

"I do." Her hands shook, but holding Uno helped remind her why she'd left. Somehow she had to be strong enough. When Tony strode over and gripped her chin, she yelped. "Let me go."

"See, you left. You took a bunch of my money and left. I've already filed a report, you know. You have to come back or I'll have you thrown in jail."

"I didn't take your money." She dropped Uno, who scattered away with a yowl. After a moment she managed to jerk her chin away. "It was mine. I earned it, I saved it. I won't let you hit me again."

"I told you I wouldn't baby. Come on. It's you and me against the world, remember?"

"You isolated me." She closed her eyes, forcing forward Grace's words. "Cut me off from everyone. Made me see you as my world until everyone gave up on me."

"No, baby. You forget how it happened. I wouldn't ever hurt you."

"You did." He had, hadn't he?

"Shh." He tugged her close. "No, baby."

Her whole body shook as her brain and heart battled it out.

She had no idea what to do now.

* * * *

Clay put his truck in park and rubbed his hand over his face. For the entire weekend he'd managed to avoid Calliope's questions, and Regan, by spending most of the time out at the Neeley Ranch. He'd even taken the extra step of paying for a room in the bed and breakfast portion.

Anything to clear his head after what had happened at Regan's.

Nothing had worked. If anything, he felt worse than he had when he'd left her apartment on Saturday morning.

He'd known what she was hiding was big, but that she was engaged? Never mind the fact that Regan wasn't even her real name. His hands shook so hard he gripped the steering wheel tight. She'd known he'd been cheated on, and didn't think it was relevant to tell him she herself was a cheater?

Another problem was that the whole situation seemed off. When he wasn't blinded by pain and anger, something nagged at him. Why was she here, and using a different name? What did this fiancé have to do with what she was going to tell him?

For that matter, what *was* she going to tell him that morning?

He shook off the questions and opened the door. No sooner was he out of the truck when he spotted Regan headed his way with Calliope beside her and Uno's cat carrier in hand.

Tension ratcheted through every muscle, and he ground his teeth together to cover his pain. She was the first woman he'd let in since the mess of Casey, and she'd betrayed him too.

Calliope moved ahead of Regan, whose gait had become stilted. Without looking back, Calli walked up until they were shoulder to shoulder. She set her hand on his shoulder. "Easy, big brother."

"Shut up Calli. This isn't about you."

"Maybe it's not about you either, you know that?" Calli stepped away, and he heard her climbing the steps to his apartment when Regan finally made the final steps to him.

Clay couldn't even process what Calli meant; Regan's closeness overwhelmed him. Friday night he'd been fooled to believe she'd let him in. He could still remember every touch, every kiss. Unfortunately every amazing memory was covered with the crunch of gravel and her fiancé's arrival. Instead of taking time to think on Calli's words, he clenched his fists. "What?"

Regan jumped, her features pale as she almost dropped the carrier. The whole cage rattled and Uno mewled pitifully as she set it down. When she spoke it was a whisper. "I'm so sorry."

"For what? Letting me help you cheat?"

"It's not what you think."

"Not what I think? He said he's your fiancé, is he?"

With her hands free, they shook harder than they had the day he'd met her. She twisted them together so tight he thought she might break her own fingers. She hazarded a glance over her shoulder.

He followed her gaze and saw someone staring at them. A man with a baby face, dark hair, and ruddy cheeks glared at them with narrowed eyes.

She shuddered and turned back, her head lowered.

Clay frowned. "That him?"

"I guess."

"So, Mandy." He snarled the name and she winced. Guilt flared when the pain in her features hit him full force. Torment darkened her eyes to almost black and he had to clench his fists tight to keep from softening toward her. "That's your real name, right?"

"I-i-it's my given name, yes. Amanda is, I don't like it, or Mandy. Never did" She cleared her throat. "I should have told you sooner. I should have explained."

"Gee, you think?"

"I'm sorry."

"Sorry doesn't mean a load of crap anymore, does it?" He folded his arms across his chest. "I can't believe I let myself fall for it. Told myself I wouldn't let a woman pull the wool over my eyes again. I thought you were different."

"I thought I was too." She swiped at tears.

"What did you tell him?"

"Nothing. I couldn't. I don't know what he'd do." Her eyes screwed shut and she dropped her head. "I never wanted this to happen."

"Yeah, well now I wish it never had." He looked away when she sobbed. When his heart lurched, his fingers twitched as if to reach for her. He balled his hands into fists again and dropped them to his side. "Why are you here now?"

"I have to get out of here. I mean…" Again she looked over her shoulder, her hands twisting around each other again until she turned back. "Tony wants us to leave right away. I managed to get another night. He doesn't like Uno— I mean, I don't want Uno around him. She doesn't deserve that."

Clay frowned and focused on the carrier at their feet. "Wait. What?"

"She doesn't deserve that. I just—I hoped you'd take her." Her voice dropped so low he almost didn't hear her whisper, "she loves you."

What was left of his heart shattered and he stepped back. "You want me to take her?"

"Or find her a good home." She backed up. "I can't take her. I have to go."

Confusion took over, and then disappointment. "That's it? That's all I get?"

"I'm sorry." Regan stopped where she was, her back to him. After a few minutes of silence, she turned back. Tears streaked down her cheeks. "I told you the reason why I picked Uno. Do you remember?"

"Yeah. You said you were alike."

"Broken." She folded her arms across her chest. "She wasn't a stray. Her missing ear wasn't because of a street cat fight. She was someone's pet that was rescued due to abuse. The owner's teenage son cut her ear clean off."

Clay's jaw dropped when she turned on her heel and darted across the street without checking the traffic well. When her fiancé wrapped his arm around Regan's shoulder, Clay thought he would throw up.

Uno meowed and the door of the carrier rattled.

Clay crouched down and frowned at the small face peering out from the carrier. "You were abused, were you? You're awfully sweet for such a thing."

He glanced back toward the diner where Regan still lingered in the parking lot. Tony, that's what Regan had called him, had a hand on her arm. He leaned in close and Regan nodded furiously, her hands raised as if in defense.

Maybe it's not about you either. Calli's words came back to him in a rush.

Clay rose to his feet and stared down the pair. Every second he watched, Regan wilted more until she almost sagged against the man. Tony ushered her into his car, then paused long enough to glare at Clay before getting in the driver's side.

Once the car left the parking lot of Myrtle's, Clay gathered the carrier and tore up the stairs to his apartment. Inside Calli greeted him with a beer, and pried the carrier from his hand. "Have a drink. I want to see this pitiful little thing."

Clay sat on a stool at the bar, unable to speak while Calli removed the cat and gushed over her. Rather than confront the conversation yet, he drank down as much of his beer as he could. Upset as his stomach was, it wasn't much.

"You went and put your foot in your mouth, didn't you?" Calli held the cat above her, making kissy faces at it, but he had no doubt she was talking to him.

"What she did—"

"She withheld information, she didn't tell you about that asshole out there, blah blah blah. Then again, you went back on your word, didn't you?"

"Excuse me?"

"You said she could tell you in her own time."

"We slept together. I helped her cheat."

"Cheat?"

"She's engaged! He called himself her fiancé, and she didn't deny it!"

Calli tsked and shook her head, gathering Uno close to her chest. "Darling, I don't know what universe you live in, but when a girl moves halfway across the country and starts going by a different name, I don't think any man she leaves behind has any right to that title."

"She said…"

Instead of pushing him for more, she scratched the cat's ear and forehead. "You're such a cutie. No wonder Regan took you in, you sweet thing. Yes you are. She likes lost causes, just like Clay over there. Clueless as the day is long, you know that?"

"She took Uno in because they were alike."

"Hear that click? I think it's the light bulb in my dim brother's brain turning on. My goodness, the man does know how to think."

"Then made it a point to tell me Uno lost her ear to abuse. Calli? What do you know?"

"Not much." Calli let Uno leap onto the table. "It's not like Regan and I had deep, serious conversations. I just speculated, and I wasn't the only one. Myrtle did, too. We both thought the worst after that creep showed up looking for her. Then you went and disappeared at the ranch, and we put the pieces of the puzzle together. After all, you didn't come home Friday night, and bozo went to Regan's early enough on Saturday."

"How'd you know?"

"You remember what I was like in high school? When I was dating that buffoon Leamon?"

Clay didn't have to think too hard to remember. Everyone in the family had been unhappy when she'd started dating Leamon. He wrinkled his nose and nodded. "You were quiet, withdrawn. It was eerie. Wait, did that asshole hit you?"

"No. There are other ways to hurt someone." Calli sat at the next stool and leaned on the bar. She reached over to grab the bowl of chips from the counter and set it between them. "That boy used to just verbally berate me. Made me feel the size of a flea most times."

"Asshole."

"Took me a long time to realize it, too. Man, you all started to give up on me. I wouldn't listen to you when you said he was a jerk. I was horrible to mom when she tried to keep me from date nights. I actually started to think he was right."

He worked his jaw in circles. "Regan—I mean, Mandy—no, Regan. She's only had three boyfriends. If she met him in high school."

"She's what, twenty two?"

"Twenty three." Bile rose so fast he had to stand. He paced and took a large swig of beer to try to get control of his thoughts. "The past few weeks were pretty amazing."

"I noticed."

"Shit, I screwed up big time."

"No, not yet. You were blindsided. What you did is forgivable, so long as you take action, big brother. Otherwise she'll be gone tomorrow one way or another."

"What's that supposed to mean?"

Calli took his beer and finished it off. She shrugged. "Let's just say if I wasn't able to pull your head out of your ass, Myrtle and I had an escape plan ready for her if she was willing to take it. Wasn't easy, neither. That scumbag wouldn't let her out of his sight."

"What do I do?"

"You give her a chance to explain."

"How? If I see that guy I'm gonna punch first, ask questions second."

"Fun as that would be, he'd call the police faster than you could get her out of there. Just leave it up to me." Calli patted his chest. "We'll get you fixed up."

"What do we do about him?"

"Odds are, if she knows she's got people behind her, she'll continue to stand up to him. She did manage to leave town on him once. Someone helped her get a backbone, we just need to make damn sure she keeps it."

Chapter Eleven

Regan paced in front of her coffee table. Any minute now they'd be leaving, and she could hardly keep still at the thought. A few weeks ago she would have gone back without a second thought, but she'd had a taste of something. Something pretty damn good.

Then she'd managed to ruin it like she did everything. Her stomach churned when she thought of how Clay had looked at her the day before. Maybe she did deserve this after all.

When he'd seen Clay's hat in the closet, Tony had decided she had nothing of worth to take with them back to Illinois. She'd be leaving her apartment with nothing but the clothes on her back. At least she had clothes in Illinois.

Tony appeared in the doorway, rubbing a towel through his damp hair. "Stop pacing. It's getting on my nerves."

"Sorry." She stopped and sank to sit on the coffee table.

He tossed aside the towel and crossed to the couch for his shirt. After her night with Clay, all she could think of was how unattractive Tony had become. Much as she loathed the idea of running another time, Myrtle's offer became more appealing by the minute.

For the time being she considered herself lucky he hadn't hit her again. Granted, he'd only hit her once six months before, but if he'd learned what she did with Clay there's no telling what he would have done.

Still, Tony's most powerful weapon was his words. He knew right to hit her where it counted, and after her visit with Clay to give him Uno, all of Tony's words seemed like a dagger in her heart. *You liked him didn't you? What an idiot. He could never like someone like you.*

Turned out Tony was right. After all, she was a liar and a cheat. Her nostrils burned with the tears she held back. Maybe going to Myrtle's wasn't such a good idea.

"Let's go." Tony hooked his hand around her arm and tugged her harshly to her feet. "I'll let you stop and say bye to your friends. Might as well get another look at that blonde before we go."

If she had any joy left inside, Regan might have scoffed. He could look all he wanted, but he had less of a chance with Calli than Regan did with Clay. Somehow she doubted Clay's sister would turn straight for the likes of Tony.

Even though he only held her elbow, Tony kept it in a vice-like grip all the way to the car. All the leading around he'd been doing with her had left a bruise on her elbow. As ordered, she'd covered it with makeup while he showered, but now she felt like rubbing it off. Maybe if she fought him he'd hit her, and then she'd have something to fight for.

But she had nothing to fight for. Clay wished he'd never met her, and she'd signed the termination of lease with Mrs. Bell. She dropped into the passenger seat and buckled the seat belt. By the time she turned back around, he'd slammed the door, so she stared out the window.

Still, maybe there was some hope. It had been bits and pieces, but Myrtle and Calli had given her a sliver of a possibility if she dared to take it. That's why they were heading to the diner now.

Tony had been vehemently opposed, until Calli got a hold of him. Regan was sure Calli could charm the fangs right out of a snake, and charm she had. Somehow she'd convinced Tony to agree to let Regan come back the next day to say goodbye to the friends she'd made.

Myrtle said they'd get her out if she wanted to take the chance.

Biggest problem was, it would mean running again. After what happened in Lake Point, and Tony finding her anyway, she wondered if it was worth it. She'd never be able to relax; she'd always be looking over her shoulder.

Always.

"I agreed to this, but don't make it long. We got a long drive back to Illinois." Tony turned off the car. He hooked a finger under her chin and yanked her gaze to his. "Once we're home things can get back to normal."

Normal. Regan forced a smile and nodded. "Sure. Normal." When she got out of the car, she couldn't stop herself from glancing toward Clay's shop. She quickly ducked her head, which was easier to do because in that split second she saw no sign of him.

Rather than linger and get more deeply depressed by it, she jogged around the car. She didn't wait for Tony to grab her elbow again, rushing forward and into The Diner quickly. The last thing she wanted to do was cry again, but the moment she saw Myrtle, the tears sprang up.

"Now don't you start that on me, child." Myrtle wagged her finger. "There'll be none of those just yet."

Regan smiled when the older woman cupped her face and wiped the tears off her cheeks with her thumbs. "I just don't like the thought of not seeing you again."

"Hush. Don't you worry so much." Myrtle smiled and nodded. "Now, Roni is in the back waiting on her goodbyes. You get a move on. I expect a good hug."

"Roni's in the back?" Regan couldn't keep the surprise from her voice, unsure why Roni would be in the kitchen when she didn't work there. At Myrtle's meaningful look, Regan realized her error. That was her escape, if she wanted it.

"Oh, go on." The familiar southern lilt of Calli made her turn around. Calli grinned and winked. "But you'd best hurry up so's I can get a nice big hug out of you girl."

Tony's frown faded a smidge with the appearance of Clay's sister. Still, he eyed Regan with a careful look. "Five minutes, Mandy. We've got to get on the road."

Regan backed away from Tony, but paused near Myrtle. When Calli swept Tony's attention away, Regan's pulse raced. She didn't want to run anymore, but she turned and bolted into the kitchen anyway. Maybe she could at least find her own courage.

She pressed her hand to her forehead and tried to gather her wits about her. What was it about Tony's presence that made her forget everything she'd done to get away? Why did she feel like she had to go back? None of it made sense.

Her breath came in small gasps as the enormity of the decision ahead of her sank in. As had become her habit, she made a beeline for the freezer. Before she could reach it, a familiar tall figure stepped in front of it.

A strangled yelp burst from Regan's belly and she stumbled back. She blinked a few times to make sure she was seeing straight before she dared lift her gaze again. Inch by inch she trailed up Clay's lean frame.

He held out a hand to her. "We have to talk."

Regan glanced over her shoulder toward the dining area.

"Please."

Much as she might not deserve life with Tony, she sure as hell didn't deserve a man like Clay. She shook her head. "No. You were right. There's nothing to talk about."

"I was hurt. I shouldn't have been so harsh."

"Harsh?" She scoffed and turned back to him. "You call what you said harsh? That was nothing, trust me. I've heard worse."

"So I gathered." Clay kept his hand held out toward her. "Please."

"I can't. I can't, not again. I'm sorry."

"Please." He stepped closer, then closer still until he brushed his fingers down her arms. "Just a few minutes. Come with me. Calli will keep him distracted and you can tell me what you wanted to tell me yesterday."

"Why?"

"Because you deserve a chance."

"No, I don't."

"Yes, you do." He cupped her cheek. "I went back on my word. I told you I'd let you tell me in your own time. I was too hurt and angry to see what you wanted me to see."

"It doesn't matter." She couldn't put any force behind the words, she wanted it to matter. Clay's gentle touch had reawakened her hope. Unfortunately, a strong dose of fear kept it from building too high. "It's too late."

"It's never too late." He took a shaky breath. "Can you forgive me?"

"Forgive you?"

"Yes."

"I…"

Tony's voice interrupted. "Mandy?"

When Calli called out to Tony to distract him again, Clay pulled her to the back door. He led her outside and closed the door behind them.

Regan followed him down the steps, but at the bottom her hand lingered on the rail. When Clay gave a gentle tug, she glanced at The Diner once more before she let go and turned to follow Clay. Maybe it wasn't too late after all.

* * * *

Clay laced his fingers with hers, but didn't push for Regan to talk. The further they got from The Diner, the more she relaxed. By the time they'd gotten several blocks away and to the frozen custard shop, she let out a long breath.

"I don't know where to start," she whispered.

"Why don't you start by telling me what flavor?"

"What?" Her eyes widened as she realized where they were. "Oh, okay. Um, I like it simple. Vanilla soft serve with rainbow sprinkles. Maybe I shouldn't. He's going to be looking for me."

"And you're with me." He squeezed her hand. "If you want to be."

"It's not that simple." She pulled her hand free and walked away.

He jogged behind her until he could fall into step with her. When they reached the next intersection he guided her to the left toward the lake. "So then start at the beginning."

"We started dating in high school. He was my first, and only until you." Her cheeks darkened, and she folded her arms across her chest.

"When did he start hurting you?"

"Depends on your definition."

Clay wanted to just pull her close and tell her it was over, but he knew it was far from over. He took a deep breath and gestured toward the woods. "Let's go to the gazebo. It should be nice and quiet this time of day."

She nodded and started down the trail ahead of him. Once there she sat and shoved her hands between her knees. She rubbed them together and shivered like she was cold despite the heat of the day. "I don't know that my family ever liked him, neither did my friends. I guess I didn't realize how much until they were out of my life."

"How did that happen?"

"Like everything else—gradually." She freed her hands, but used them to grip the edge of the bench. Instead of looking at him, she stared at her sneakers. "I mostly didn't realize it had happened. I went from annoyance to my parents to complete isolation from them. Same with my friends. Eventually I was a hermit, Tony was all I had."

He moved closer on the bench, but didn't push his luck and dare to touch her yet. "Calli suggested verbal abuse."

"I've had a lot of time to think about that. Grace, who helped me get out, she helped me figure it out. When he's not around I see it clearer." She tilted her head and stared into the trees. "Emotional mostly at first. Isolating me from those that didn't like him, making sure I knew it was my fault, not his. That he was the only one that wouldn't leave."

"Did your parents try to tell you?"

"No." She sighed long and low. "Long story short, he was all I had until he wanted more things and made me get a job. That's how I met Grace. I wouldn't associate with anyone at first, but Grace was the only one that pushed the issue."

"I'd like to meet her and thank her."

She glanced at him, a hint of a smile forming. "Maybe she recognized herself in me, she was once in the same place as I was. She ran, too. Told me how and helped me save the money to do it. If it wasn't for her, I wouldn't be here."

"Did he hit you?"

"Once. That's when I knew I had to leave. For some reason I was fine with everything else, but when he hit me, something snapped. I had to get out. Apparently, I didn't go far enough."

"I think you did." He set his hand on hers, relieved she didn't pull away. "I know there's more, probably lots more."

She nodded and pulled her gaze away again. "But he's probably looking for me."

"It took guts to leave."

"I missed him, you know. After I left. Maybe I don't have guts, after all."

"You left. You can stay gone. You can stay where you belong."

"I don't belong anywhere." She pulled her hand free from his and rose.

He followed suit, but set his hands on her shoulders. While he wanted to make things right between them, he couldn't do that until she was able to stand up for herself. "I think you're stronger than you give yourself credit for. I also think you know where you belong. Just like I knew when I first came here, you know you belong here in Lake Point."

"I'm not strong. If I was, I would have told you. I should have told you."

"I should have trusted you."

"I can't stand up to him. I never could."

"You've been alone. You're not alone any longer." When she turned around, he didn't waver from her tear filled gaze. He kept his hands on her shoulders and nodded. "I'll go with you, and Calli and Myrtle will be there. You don't have to do what he tells you to do. You don't have to do what anyone tells you to do, Regan."

She smiled through her tears. "You called me Regan."

"It's your name, isn't it?"

"Yes."

"Are you going to stay?"

"You'll stand with me?"

"I'll kick him out on his sorry ass if he gives you any trouble."

"What about…"

He brushed a stray lock of hair behind her ear. "We'll figure that out later. First things first—you have to remember how strong you are."

"I'll try."

"There is no try."

Again, her smile lit up her features. "Geek."

"Takes one to know one."

* * * *

Regan braced herself as she pulled open the door to The Diner. Before it was halfway open she heard Tony ranting inside. The moment she started to tremble, a strong hand settled on the small of her back. She found Clay's warm gray eyes and smiled her thanks.

"Stop yelling, Tony. Myrtle has customers." Regan would have cringed at the tremor of her voice, but Calli's grin boosted her confidence a little more.

"There you are, and what's this? Unhand my fiancée." Tony frowned and rose. "I think you've toyed her with her enough."

"Clay hasn't done anything wrong." Her hand shook, but she managed to get the ring off her finger. "And I'm not your fiancée. I left, remember?"

"You made a mistake." Tony moved closer.

"Then I guess this will be a bigger one in your eyes. Go home. Without me. I'm not leaving." Regan was sure her bones would rattle right out of her body with how much her nerves were on edge.

The moment Tony opened his mouth, Calli was at Regan's side. She laced her hand with Regan's and smiled an overly saccharine smile at Tony. "Get a clue, sugar. You're done for. You'll have to find some other poor sapling to wilt and wither under you."

"Mandy!" Tony all but barked her name and grabbed her elbow to pull her away. "Come with me and we'll talk this out, without these hicks."

"These hicks are my friends." Regan twisted against his grip. As usual, his hold didn't release so easy. "And stop that, you're hurting me."

Clay's hand clamped on Tony's wrist, and the pressure of Tony's fingers disappeared from Regan's elbow. Anger lined Clay's features even darker than the previous day as he glared daggers at Tony. "It's not right to be hurting a woman. Rumor is that's not the first time, neither. Maybe we should have your mama reteach your proper manners."

Tony winced seconds before Clay released him. "Mandy. You don't honestly think—"

"I don't care how you plan to finish that statement." Regan clenched Calli's hand tight in her own. Any second she was sure her strength would fail her, and she was happy to borrow Calli's. "I'm staying."

Tony looked between the three, and then his gaze circled the restaurant and his eyes widened. That was when Regan noticed some of her regular customers on their feet, heading toward their little group.

Calli leaned in and muttered, "Guess you got friends."

"I'd forgotten what that was like," Regan whispered back. She lifted her chin. "Just go, Tony. Sell the ring, sell my stuff. I've got a new life here. I'm not your Mandy anymore. I'm Regan, and I belong here."

Whatever protest Tony wanted to make was cut off when Clay pushed him to the door. Once Tony was outside, Clay shut the door and stood in front of it.

Regan released Calli's hand and edged toward the door as well. When Tony got back in his car, she laced her hand with Clay's.

He leaned toward her. "So I'm guessing tomorrow night's going to be one hell of a celebration. Mind if I ask to be your date for it?"

"What? Why tomorrow night?"

"It's the fourth of July, silly. Independence Day? Seems awful fitting."

Independence Day. She sure liked the sound of it. Then it hit her what he'd asked. She turned to meet his gaze as tires squealed in the parking lot. "You want to be my date?"

"If you'll have me."

"You want me? I'm broken, you know."

"Who's your favorite character in Star Trek?"

She smiled, her heart fluttering. "All of them."

"Then you'll do just fine."

Epilogue

Regan fought the urge to yawn. If she did, Clay might help along her desire to just report to the hotel and do this tomorrow.

"Are you sure you're ready for this?" As if reading her mind, Clay set his hand on hers as he asked the question. With his other hand, he guided the truck off the interstate.

"Turn left here, then right at the first light. And yes, I'm sure." The past year had been at turns wonderful and very difficult. She could still hardly believe that just two nights before she'd celebrated her second Independence Day with Clay.

Together they'd cuddled on a blanket watching the fireworks over the lake until the last ember had fallen from the sky. After that they'd lingered despite their planned early morning.

So much had changed since she'd first arrived in Lake Point, Regan really did feel like a different person. With Myrtle's advice, she'd found a good therapist that worked on a sliding scale so it didn't break Regan financially.

Thanks to Clay's urging, she'd gone to see Ivy and ended up teaching a small class a few months back. Ivy promised her more classes next year if she wanted them, and Regan definitely did. She enjoyed teaching, it turned out.

Her relationship with Clay had gotten deeper. At first, after Tony had finally left town, they'd gone back to almost the start of their relationship again. They dated some and took it slow until she'd been in therapy for a while. The most amazing part about it for her was that even now, when they'd been in a definite serious relationship for three months, Clay was always a friend first.

Unlike what she'd known for so long, he pushed her to go hang out with Roni or let Calli drag her out on some insane adventure that always ended in a story to tell. Best part was that he wanted to hear the story every time.

Regan smiled and squeezed Clay's hand. "Are you sure you want to come along? I don't know what's going to happen. Turn left at that weird lawn ornament."

"What the hell is that thing?" Clay turned his head to eye it while he waited for an opening in traffic.

"I never did figure that out. I was wondering if it was still here."

"It looks like a rooster, but then there's that weird horse head."

"Coming out of the tail feathers. I know. I stopped asking long ago."

Clay made the left, still shaking his head. "And yes, I'm sure. I want to be there if you need me to be."

"You always are." She sighed. "Turn right at the next street."

"Gotcha."

"Have I told you yet today that I love you?"

"Maybe once or twice, but I don't mind hearing it again."

"Well then, I love you. Thank you."

"Love you too, and stop thanking me. No need."

"The blue house with the white birch in the front yard." Her hand shook when she reached for the door handle, and she took a shaky breath.

Rather than pull into the driveway, he parked across the street against the curb. He tugged her close and kissed her temple. "If you'd rather get to a hotel, shower and relax, we can. This will still be here tomorrow."

"I showered this morning and it's only been a couple of hours, but thank you for the excuse." She met his gaze. "If I wait longer, I'll chicken out."

"A girl that can dance onstage at Rocky Horror doesn't know the meaning of chicken out." He gave her a gentle kiss. "Then let's go. I'll be right here with you."

"I know." She let him pull her out of the truck through the driver's side. On the street, she adjusted her top and brushed away an imaginary wrinkle before she took his hand. "Is my hair messed up? My makeup?"

"You look beautiful." When he said it, she almost believed it.

Almost, but not quite. She'd need a little more therapy for that. Well, therapy, and for today to go well. "I'm suddenly not sure."

Clay wrapped his arm around her waist and held her close as they walked to the door. "I have a feeling it's going to be fine. Just take a deep breath. Want me to knock?"

Regan shook her head and reached out to push the bell. The doorbell rang, followed by the deep bark of a Labrador. She smiled. "I guess they got a new dog after Spooky died."

"Pet lovers always do." Clay himself had gotten a dog. When Regan ended up staying in Lake Point, she'd taken Uno back into her apartment, and Clay claimed loneliness, even though he'd only had Uno for a few days. He got a beagle and had named her Columbia. Regan still blushed when he hinted at telling someone why he'd picked that name.

A familiar woman's voice hollered at the dog to hush up before the door cracked open. "No, Ebony. Get back."

Regan's breath caught in her throat, and she tightened her hold on Clay when her mother finally turned their way.

Time had hardly touched her mother's features, just a few more lines around the eyes. Her hair was dyed red to cover the grays she'd had as long as Regan could remember. Deep brown eyes grew wide and she shook her head. "My God. Amanda? John! It's Amanda!"

"Hi, Mom."

The End

Up next in Holidays in Lake Point

Witch Way

Chapter One

Even from across the street and behind the fire departments barriers, the heat of the house fire stirred Felicity's hair like a breeze. She held her camera close and circled around for a better shot. The family gathered near the ambulance. The whole family had come out safe, but when Felicity raised her camera to get the shot of the EMT tending to them, the little girl shrieked long and loud.

Everyone in the vicinity jumped when she started calling for her dog. Felicity turned her attention back to the house that was no doubt a total loss, although the fire department had impressively kept the damage to the nearby houses at a minimum. The first story of the house still appeared less damaged, but once they accounted for water and collapsing floors, it would be gone for sure. She sighed at the realization she'd become all too familiar with since she'd started working the fire beat.

As she snapped a few pictures of the neighboring house, another call went out through the crowd. Felicity lowered the camera in time to see a firefighter emerge from the house with the dog in question in his arms.

Unable to avoid the good story, or the nagging feeling this fireman was new, she darted to the end of the barricades. She nudged through the crowd and dropped to her knees to get under the barrier to get the shot. When the fireman tossed aside his mask and began CPR on the pooch, she snapped away quick as she could.

CPR on a pooch. You're going to make headlines, buddy. Not once did she stop taking pictures. While for some time now she'd wished to be the one in front of the cameras down the street, doing what she did now allowed her to sneak into the heat of the story much better.

After five minutes the dog jerked and squirmed. They actually put an oxygen mask on it and got it back to the family. Felicity rose and managed to get a few more shots of the back of the fireman's head. "Come on, turn around. Let me get the hero's close up."

When he did turn, she almost dropped her camera. "Shit."

The man facing her was one she hadn't seen in years. Not since she'd been a gangly teen he and his twin called her 'pencil prick' on a regular basis, tormenting her alongside her stupid cousin. Nowadays this man was a far cry better than the teenage boy he'd been.

Even with soot covering his features and the dark night, she could tell he had something about him. Her libido kicked into high gear, but when she took a step forward to go to him—for the story, of course—a bulky, short man blocked her path.

"Felicity." The chief's voice was muffled behind his mask when he stepped in front of her. "Behind the barrier. You know the rules."

Out of habit, she grabbed her voice recorder and clicked it on. "Where are you in the fight now, Chief?"

"It's about containment now. You've been on enough of these to know that."

"But an official statement is always better, Chief." Felicity smiled bright, though her eyes kept darting to the not-so-new guy.

"Fine. The house is a total loss. Right now we're working to minimize the damage to the surrounding homes while the fire burns itself out. No one in the family was seriously hurt. Just some smoke inhalation."

"And what about your new hero? The dog rescuer?" She nodded toward the man in question, and was pleased to see him return the nod. *I wonder if he remembers me. I sure remember him.*

"Craig MacAlister. Just transferred in from Wyoming County." The Chief pulled off his mask. "He heard the dog and pulled it out of its cage. The dog is going to need to be checked by a vet to see if it'll survive its ordeal."

"You mean he transferred back here from Wyoming County. He's from here, isn't he?"

"Yes. Lake Point born and raised. We've welcomed him back with open arms."

"Thank you, Chief." She kept her gaze on Craig. "Can I talk to the hero?"

"When we're done, Felicity. Now get back behind the barrier and let us finish our jobs."

"Of course." She ducked under the sawhorse that served as a barrier, never taking her eyes off Craig for a second. Years ago he'd tormented the hell out of her, but that was the past, and right now she could use a hero.

Or rather, she'd be happy to have a hero use her.

She shook her head to clear the thoughts even as he was led to the ambulance and an oxygen mask, still staring right back at her. Once the fire was contained she'd find out if he remembered her. Whether he did or not, she'd make sure he knew her now.

About the Author

Sarah Cass' world is regularly turned upside down by her three special needs kids and loving mate, so she breaks genre barriers; dabbling in horror, straight fiction and urban fantasy. She loves historicals and romance, and characters who are real and flawed, so she writes to understand what makes her fictional people tick. And she lives for a happy ending – eventually. And enough twists to make it look like she enjoys her title of Queen of Trauma Drama a little too much.

An ADD tendency leaves her with a variety of interests that include singing, dancing, crafting, cooking, and being a photographer. She fights through the struggles of the day, knowing the battles are her crucible; she may emerge scarred, but always stronger. The rhythms to her activities drive her words forward, pushing her through the labyrinths of the heart and the nightmares of the mind, driving her to find resolutions to her characters' problems.

While busy creating worlds and characters as real to her as her own family, she leads an active online life with her blog, Redefining Perfect, which gives a real and sometimes raw glimpse into her life and art. You can most often find her popping out her 140 characters in Twitter speak, and on Facebook.

Books by Sarah Cass
The Tribe Series
The Tribe
The Wolf
The Chief
The Raven
The Dominion Falls Series
Changing Tracks
Derailed
Dark Territory
Runaway Train
Home Signal
The Lake Point Series
Santa, Maybe
Deep-Fried Sweethearts
Stalled Independence
Witch Way
A Thorough Thanksgiving
Eve's New Year
Heartstrings & Hockey Pucks
Luck of the Cowgirl
Stars, Stripes & Motorbikes
Free Falling
Love for Hire
Stand Alone Novels
Masked Hearts
Leap

Divine Roses Ink